ATTACK OF THE KILLER TOMATOES

JEFF STRAND

BASED ON THE SCREENPLY BY
COSTA DILLON, JOHN DEBELLO, & STEPHEN PEACE

Encyclopocalypse Publications
www.encyclopocalypse.com

PREFACE

On October 8th, 1978, a motion picture was released that would change cinema history forever. *Attack of the Killer Tomatoes* was met with instant critical acclaim, with Leonard Maltin proclaiming that "it makes *Casablanca* look like *Exorcist II: The Heretic*." Siskel & Ebert suggested that they would need thumb-enhancement surgery to sufficiently convey the intensity of their two thumbs up. (Though Ebert backed out, Siskel did in fact get the surgery, spending the remainder of his life with a grotesquely oversized thumb that was prone to infection.) When critic Pauline Kael wrote a review giving it a mere three stars out of four, suggesting that it wasn't quite as amazing as everybody said, readers were so enraged that they burned down her home with her still inside, and she remains dead to this day.

Attack of the Killer Tomatoes was nominated for nine Academy Awards but only won five, including Best Foreign Language Film, a category it qualified in because of the language spoken by the tomatoes. The previous year, *Star Wars* had won an Oscar for Visual

Effects; in an unprecedented move, the award was rescinded, because the sheer spectacle of *Attack of the Killer Tomatoes* made Academy voters realize that George Lucas' film was unworthy of the honor.

Even today, *Attack of the Killer Tomatoes* (hereafter abbreviated to *Attack of...Killer Tomatoes*) tops almost every list of the finest motion pictures ever produced. While classics like *Gone with the Wind* have lost their luster, *Attack of...Killer Tomatoes* is timeless, revealing new layers of thematic depth with every viewing. It's not just that the tomatoes are a metaphor. It's that every individual tomato is a separate metaphor.

And yet there has never been a novelization.

Pulitzer-prize winning author James Michener had been hired to write one, but found the project too challenging and returned his seven-figure advance after three years of struggle. The project circulated through the publishing community for decades. Judy Blume claimed to have finished it, but an FBI raid on her home revealed that she had only written half of the first chapter. The world became despondent. It is said that Queen Elizabeth II threatened to "start chopping off some [*expletive deleted*] heads if I don't get my [*expletive deleted*] tomato novel," though some scholars feel this is apocryphal.

My first involvement with the project came about twenty years ago, when I had a meeting with the movie's screenwriters, Costa Dillon, John DeBello, and Steve Peace to discuss writing a book version of their masterpiece. They laughed in my face. I mean that they said, "Move your face closer...closer...a little closer...there you go!" and then literally laughed in it. Flecks of spittle from all three of them struck my nose and chin. I walked out of the meeting with tears of shame burning their way down my cheeks like rivers of lava.

I vowed revenge, then remembered that I'm too lazy for such things. I forgot all about it until last year, when I made an astonishing discovery: *a novelization had been written and never published.*

Yes, Ebeneezer Tomatobookwriter had written it in 1979. ("Tomatobookwriter" was his real name, and it actually dates back to the 16th century. Ebezeener told me that he didn't even notice the coincidence until he was nearly finished with the book.)

When I visited his home, he showed me the manuscript, bound in gold.

"Why didn't you ever publish it?" I asked.

"It would always be my greatest achievement," he explained. "I couldn't let my career peak so soon. I needed to wait until I knew it would be my final work."

"Are you near death?" I asked.

"Oh, goodness no," he said. "I've got at least thirty or forty more years in me."

And in that moment I asked myself: was I prepared to take a human life? For the third time? Yes, indeed I was. I beat Ebeneezer Tomatobookwriter to death with the very manuscript you're reading right now.

As I write these words, I'll admit that I'm questioning the wisdom of confessing to first degree murder right here in the foreword. Also, maybe I shouldn't be blabbing that I'm trying to pass a dead man's work off as my own. I might regret it later. But I'm feeling kind of privileged and invulnerable, and I don't feel like rewriting this whole thing, so I will let it stand.

Anyway, here it is, the novelization of *Attack of...Killer Tomatoes*, hereafter expanded to *Attack of the Killer Tomatoes* to boost the word count. I hope you enjoy it, and I will wallow in despair if you don't.

Jeff Strand
Beardmore Glacier, Antarctica

MANDATORY SING-A-LONG

Attaaaack of the killer tomatoes
Attaaaack of the killer tomatoes
They'll beat you, bash you, squish you,
mash you
Chew you up for brunch
And finish you off for dinner or lunch.

They're marching down the halls
They're crawling up the walls
They're gooey, gushy, squishy, mushy
Rotten to the core
They're standing outside your door.

Remember Herman Farbage
While taking out his garbage
He turned around and he did see
Tomatoes hiding in his tree
Now he's just a memory.

I know I'm going to miss her
A tomato ate my sister
Sacramento fell today

They're marching into San Jose
Tomatoes are on their way.

The mayor is on vacation
The governor's fled the nation
The police have gone on strike today
The National Guard has run away
Tomatoes will have their day.

And I can see you fear-squirm
This song is now an earworm
It will never leave your head
Until the day that you are dead
Wish you'd read something else instead

Attaaaack of the killer tomatoes
Attaaaack of the killer tomatoes
They'll beat you, bash you, squish you,
mash you
Chew you up for brunch
And finish you off for dinner or lunch
Lunch, lunch
Dinner or lunch, lunch, lunch
Dinner or luuuuuunch

CHAPTER 1

Present day (1978)

As she did the dishes, Penelope thought about her childhood friend Herman Farbage. Because kids were always on the lookout for names that rhymed with words that could generate quick and easy insults, he'd gone through life being called Herman *Garbage*. (Though, surprisingly, children never thought to take it to the next level with *Vermin* Garbage.) So the fact that he'd died while taking out his garbage was a cruel irony.

Something caught Penelope's attention.

A whole tomato in the sink. She didn't remember dropping it in there. In fact, to the best of her knowledge, the entire kitchen had been devoid of tomatoes. Her husband Chuck wasn't the kind of person who would leave a red, ripe tomato sitting in the sink. She thought about each of her three children: Reginald, Daphne, and her favorite, Elaine. None of them would just leave a tomato in the sink, either; not even Daphne, her least favorite of the three. Not to mention that Chuck was at work and the kids were at school, and if the tomato had been there since this morning, she would've noticed it while doing the dishes.

Hmmm. Most peculiar indeed. The only logical explanation was that she was off her meds and hallucinating, which was a source of concern but could wait until the housework was done.

The tomato began to move.

Impossible! Tomatoes didn't move unless they were manually rolled, placed upon an incline, or pelted at somebody.

It rolled in a circle around the edge of the garbage disposal.

No! This couldn't be happening! This violated the laws of tomato physics! This was absolute madness that could not be explained by science of the past, present, or future! Penelope wanted to drop to the kitchen floor, curl into the fetal position, and scream at the top of her lungs until the insanity went away, but instead she continued to gape at the sink.

The tomato began to speak.

Not human speech. Nothing like "Howdy, ma'am, I'm a tomato." Just gibberish.

And then it bounced out of the sink, launching its circular form directly at her.

Penelope's parents had never instilled in her a fear of tomatoes. It hadn't been necessary. They were so small. So harmless. Who, deathly allergies notwithstanding, had ever been hurt by a tomato? You were far more likely to accidentally cut yourself dicing one than you were to be attacked by the tomato itself.

Were they gross on the inside? Sure. But so were humans, if you really thought about it.

Because Penelope had not been trained from an early age to distrust tomatoes, her reflexes were slow.

The tomato smacked directly into the center of her forehead.

Then it dropped to the kitchen floor, where it didn't splatter as much as she would've hoped.

The tomato launched itself at her again. But how? It had no legs! It had no wings!

Penelope cried out in pain as the tomato smacked into her stomach.

Once again it dropped to the kitchen floor, unsquished. It babbled at her. Penelope thought it was saying: *Just stay calm, my darling, and await the sweet release of death*, but she didn't speak tomato and couldn't tell for certain.

No. She would not await the sweet release of death. All manner of vegetables, from artichokes to zucchini, had been chopped up and cooked in this very kitchen. Not once had the tables been turned on the humans, and sentient or not, this tomato wasn't going to change that.

It launched itself at Penelope again. This time, she ducked out of the way.

"Ha!" she shouted. "Not so—"

The tomato bounced off the wall and struck her in the face. Penelope lost her balance and fell to the floor. The tomato quickly rolled toward her, babbling with homicidal intent.

Penelope sat up. Gritting her teeth and summoning every ounce of strength that she could manage after her minor tumble, she got back to her feet before the tomato could bump into her.

She stood next to the counter. The counter contained drawers. The drawers contained kitchen utensils. Amongst the kitchen utensils were knives.

She opened the nearest drawer. It was full of dish towels and oven mitts. Argh! She should've known not to choose that drawer. But she wasn't doomed yet; there was still time to open at least one more drawer.

The tomato bashed into her ankle, making her cry out.

Penelope opened the second-nearest drawer. This one was filled with knives. Enough knives that Daphne often said, "Jeez, Mom, why do we have so many knives in this drawer? People are going to think we're a family of serial killers!" It was not the reason Daphne was Penelope's least-favorite child—that was a hair-color issue—but it didn't help.

Because the tomato was actively bashing into her legs, Penelope did not have an opportunity to thoroughly review the knife selection and determine which one was best suited for tomato defense. She just grabbed one. A steak knife. The perfect tool to kill a *beefsteak* tomato.

"Die!" she screamed, crouching down and thrusting the knife toward the tomato.

It rolled out of the way in the nick of time.

"Die!" she screamed again, thrusting the knife toward the tomato's new location.

It rolled out of the way, again in the nick of time.

Penelope decided that perhaps screaming "Die!" was cluing the tomato in about when she planned to strike. So she crouched casually for a few moments, hoping the tomato would think that she'd decided there was no compelling reason to try to stab it again.

She thrust the knife at it.

The tomato rolled out of the way in the nick of time.

Then it launched itself at her again. Somehow Penelope knew this attack was different. This time, the tomato would not just bounce off. This time, Penelope, like Herman Farbage before her, would meet her tragic fate.

Penelope screamed and screamed.

———

The official dead body photographer took pictures of Penelope as a pair of detectives studied the crime scene. There was no evidence of foul play, and the majority of household accidents occurred in the kitchen, but Harry always hated to call something an accident. It just seemed lazy.

"What do you make of it?" asked Joe.

"I don't know," said Harry, writing in his notebook. "No weapons, no motive, no clothes."

"No clothes? She's clearly wearing clothes. They're right there on her dead body."

"Not in the sketch I'm making. But I have no idea how this could have happened. All we've got to go on is this bloody corpse."

Joe knelt beside the corpse, ran his finger through the blood, and tasted it. Harry had often wanted to do something like this, but had always worried that the other people on the scene would judge him for it. He admired Joe for his courage in deciding what he wanted and going for it, with no fear of the consequences.

"Look again," said Joe. "It's not blood…it's tomato juice."

"Ew. You just licked tomato juice off a corpse. That can't be sanitary."

Joe ran his finger through the liquid again and tasted it. "Definitely tomato juice. Honestly makes us look a bit silly, considering how tomato juice doesn't much resemble blood in texture or color. But we never claimed to be good detectives."

"Oh, no," said Harry. "I'm thoroughly incompetent. Heck, my badge is upside down. So what are we thinking? She ate a bad tomato?"

"Whatever gets us to the bar the quickest."

———

Phil and Agatha sat at their dining room table, silently reading the newspaper as they ate breakfast. Phil was surprised by how many tomato-themed stories were in there today. Something about a worldwide surplus, and tomatoes growing at an unusually rapid pace. It seemed like something that should concern him.

But there was also this delightful brand-new comic strip called *Garfield*, about a morbidly obese cat. Phil chuckled, imagining that a cat that size would be wheezing a lot. He hoped the strip stuck to jokes about the cat's grotesque enormity, instead of switching to far-fetched scenarios like a cat hating Mondays (cats didn't know one day of the week from another) or loving lasagna.

Phil took a sip of his coffee. Tasted like coffee.

Then he took a sip of his tomato juice. Hmmm. It didn't taste like tomato juice. It tasted like...death.

Phil gasped and clutched at his throat.

Agatha continued to read her newspaper, unaware.

Phil spat out the juice. He frantically tried to signal to his wife that he was choking.

Of course, he only *wished* he was choking. There's no reason to get into the detailed science, but he basically had *living tomato juice* inside of his body. Holy crap! Can you imagine if you drank something that was alive, and it *stayed* alive, and it was *angry*?

I know it's a bit early for the author of this novelization to start inserting himself into the action, but

ATTACK OF THE KILLER TOMATOES

the dude who drinks the tomato juice and dies in the movie version of *Attack of the Killer Tomatoes* gets, like, twenty seconds of screen time, despite his *unimaginably* horrific fate. That aspect of the tomato mythos could've been the entire movie! What was that tomato juice doing inside of his body? Was it trying to eat its way out? Did it reconstitute his DNA? I mean, oh my God! His suffering must have been legendary. It's freaking me out so much that I won't be able to drink tomato juice for at least a couple of weeks.

Anyway, I apologize for the interruption. It won't happen again. Back to the story!

Phil toppled over in his chair, spilling coffee and the rest of the tomato juice everywhere.

Finally, Agatha lowered her newspaper. "Honey, what's a six-letter word for 'Sent to one's grave' that starts with T-O-M?"

Phil did not answer.

"Oh, never mind," said Agatha. "It's *tombed*."

She reached for her coffee. The cup had toppled over. Not that Phil had bothered to say anything about it—it was just like that man to not notice that coffee had spilled all over the tablecloth.

He wasn't even sitting at the table anymore. It was just like that man to be so rude that he left the breakfast table without excusing himself.

"Phil!" she called out. "You spilled our coffee!"

He didn't answer.

And then she saw him lying on the floor. He had rage-filled living tomato juice flowing through his veins, and the sight was so unimaginably ghastly that mere words cannot describe it. Not even the most skilled of writers could convey the sheer horror of the sight upon which Agatha gazed. She put her hand to her mouth, but was too frightened to scream, and not even a whisper emerged. Her brain was not prepared for the expansion of her worldview to encompass this horror, and instead settled for a black void where her mind used to be.

Agatha slumped forward, lost forever.

———

Jess lowered his copy of *Field & Stream* at the sound of glass breaking. "Look at the giant tomato, Martha," he said to his wife, Martha.

"I didn't know they grew 'em so big, Jess," said Martha, to Jess.

"I wonder where he's going?" Jess wondered to Martha.

The answer was not long in arriving.

"He got little Timmy," Jess told Martha.

"Poor Timmy," Martha remarked to Jess.

"He ate him all up," said Jess. He returned to his magazine. Jess had seen a lot in the war, and, quite honestly, a giant killer tomato gobbling down a young boy didn't really register as more than a quick curiosity.

He was dead inside, just like his wife Martha. Oh, how they longed to feel something, *anything*.

Their story was a tragic one, although not as tragic as what had just happened to Phil, who *drank living tomato juice*. Gaaaahhh!!!

CHAPTER 2

———

U.S. Department of Agriculture.
GD-3 Project Experimental Field.
No Trespassing.
Do Not Leave Your Dog Inside the Vehicle Unattended.

Bob the Pilot, whose real name wasn't Bob, knew he had a couple of VIPs in his helicopter. But he didn't care. Ned Beatty, Margot Kidder, Elvis Presley before his death last year...none of that mattered to Bob the Pilot. His job was to fly the chopper, and he was the best helicopter pilot in the entire San Diego area, if not the entire San Diego area and some outskirts. He knew what every single knob, switch, and lever did, and encouraged his passengers to test his knowledge. He'd been flying for over thirty years, and not a single person had ever fallen out in mid-air. Not one. Fewer than half of helicopter pilots could make that claim.

People could have called him Mr. Safety, although nobody ever did, much to his chagrin.

His impeccable record was why Bob the Pilot assumed that he wasn't going to crash today. The idea that they might crash honestly didn't even occur to him. In fact, they'd almost reached their destination, the U.S. Department of Agriculture GD-3 Experimental Field, where he could touch down safely, let his VIPs out of the vehicle, and then get blackout drunk.

Something flew through the air at them.

Something spherical. Something reddish orange, with a green stem at the top.

It looked a lot like a tomato, but nobody would dare fling a tomato at a helicopter. That would be a safety hazard.

It had to be a nuclear missile.

No, it was indeed a tomato.

Bob the Pilot never used unclean language. It was why people could have, but did not, call him Mr. Never Swears. Yet as the tomato struck the helicopter, Bob the Pilot uttered the "sh" part of the s-word, and though he stopped himself in time, deep in his heart he knew that it still counted.

The entire helicopter jolted.

Bob the Pilot let out another half-finished curse word as the helicopter began to spin out of control.

"What's going on?" one of the VIPs asked from the back seat.

Bob the Pilot could have been called Mr. Doesn't Ignore A Direct Question From A Passenger, and turned around to explain that a tomato had struck the helicopter, which is why they were spiraling toward the ground at a deadly speed. He sort of wished he'd used that time to try to steady the chopper.

His life flashed before his eyes, though it skipped most of the good parts.

"Are we going to die?" screamed the other VIP, not that Bob the Pilot cared which one was which.

Bob the Pilot saw no reason to calm his passengers in their final moments. "Probably, yeah."

Impact.

Darkness.

Bob the Pilot opened his eyes. He was floating above the burning wreckage of the helicopter. An angel floated beside him.

"Please," said Bob the Pilot. "I'm not ready to die. I have so many people left to transport."

"You're not dead," said the angel. "You scraped up your arm and got a bit of vomit on your pants, that's all."

"Then why are you here?"

"I wanted to watch a helicopter crash! Whooooo-eeeeee! You should've seen it! So much production value!"

"I'm still alive?"

"Yep. Although you're trapped inside the burning wreckage, so if I were you I'd fly back down to your body ASAP."

Bob the Pilot flew back down into his body. Yes, he'd wrecked a $60,000 helicopter, which probably wouldn't seem like a lot to future generations but was quite a hefty price tag in current 1978 money. But at least there were no burning corpses inside.

Jim Richardson was one of the VIPs who was not a burning corpse. He did not exit the burning aircraft into an environment of serenity, but rather pure chaos. Police sirens blared. Rifles fired. Hand grenades exploded. Bear traps snapped shut. People screamed. The tomatoes—the *killer* tomatoes—were on the attack, and there was no time to relax from a traumatic helicopter crash.

Larry Riley, the head of the Department of Agriculture, had also survived the crash, though not without a little vomit on his own pants. He and Jim hurried away from the wreckage.

"My God, did you see that?" asked Jim, frantic. "A tomato!"

"You didn't see anything, you didn't hear anything," said Larry. This wasn't true at all, but Jim assumed that Larry's words were wishful thinking rather than a statement of fact.

"The pilot's still in there!"

"Forget about the pilot!"

"We can't leave him!" Jim insisted. "Have you ever burned to death? It's a terrible way to go!"

The pilot crawled out of the wreckage and gave everybody a thumbs-up.

"See, I told you he was fine," said Larry.

"You didn't say he was fine. You said to forget about him."

"Don't act like I'm being callous just because I said to let the pilot die. You would've done the same thing."

"No! I was right here, and I literally said that we can't leave him!"

Larry shrugged. "We'll have to agree to disagree."

"It's just too incredible," said Jim, incredulously. "A kamikaze tomato!"

"Tomatoes can't fly," said Larry.

"Yeah? They can't eat people either, but they're doing one heck of an impression!"

"Oh, snap!" said the pilot to Larry, anachronistically. "You just got *schooled!*"

"Quiet, you!" Larry snarled. "Get back in the helicopter!"

"But—!"

"I said get back in the helicopter!"

The pilot sadly crawled back into the helicopter.

Larry pointed to a random sheriff. "Jim, talk to that sheriff and find out what's going on!"

Jim nodded and scurried off.

Larry waved to Ward Howderfeld, who was in some sort of position of power. "Get over here! How bad is it?"

"Well, sir, I definitely don't think it'll fly again."

"Not the helicopter, you wiener!"

Ward winced at the savage sting of the insult. He'd deserved that.

"What about the tomatoes?" Larry asked.

Ward took a moment to compose himself after being called a wiener. You didn't bounce back from that right away. "We found two more bodies at the main road, nobody famous, but we pushed the tomatoes back to the north end. I don't think any managed to escape the perimeter."

"They better not have!" said Larry. "I want this thing contained!"

"I understand, sir, thus the establishment of a perimeter. But nothing seems to stop them. We tried chemicals, bugs, bullets! Nothing works! Well, the bullets work, but you have to actually hit the tomatoes with them, and they won't stop rolling around!"

"What kind of bugs did you use?"

"Aphids, sir," said Ward. "The most dangerous tomato pest of them all."

"Regular aphids or giant mutant aphids?"

"Regular ones, sir."

"Get our men working on giant ones!"

"Won't that cause other issues down the line?"

"One problem at a time!" Larry said. "If we start worrying about the consequences of unleashing giant mutant aphids on the world, we'll never get anything done. You say the chemicals didn't work—are you sure you used enough?"

"Our crop dusters are circling as we speak, sir. One nearly hit us a few seconds ago."

"We should be drenching the tomatoes in that stuff. It's like how if you spray a little bit of Raid into your mouth it's a tasty treat, but if you drink the entire can, you've got problems. There should be *rivers* of herbicides."

"But won't that kill the humans, too?" Ward asked.

"Why must you always be thinking one step ahead? What's wrong with the step you're on now?"

"Can I come out of the helicopter now?" asked the pilot.

"Yes, that's fine," said Larry. The pilot crawled out of the burning wreckage, patted out the fires on his clothing, and was struck by the crop duster plane. Larry returned his attention to Ward. "The President wants a full investigation."

"We can't let this out," said Ward. "People would—"

"Panic, that's what!"

"Panic, right. That's much better than what I was going to say."

"And you know whose ass is on the line? Yours, mine, and the entire AG department."

Ward nodded. He had assumed that a different set

of asses were on the line, but Larry's list made a lot of sense.

"The president will get his investigation," said Larry. "But we'll keep it quiet. I've arranged for the most obscure generals, the most obscure scientists, and to head the investigation…". Larry took out a picture. "This man."

"Jim Belushi?"

"No."

"Then I don't recognize him," said Ward.

"Nobody does. His name is Mason Dixon."

"Like the line?"

"What line? Anyway, he hasn't worked since the Bay of Pigs."

A very amusing image of a bay filled with pigs popped into Ward's mind. But then he remembered that 112 human beings lost their lives and 360 were wounded in the Bay of Pigs, and it wasn't really appropriate fodder for humor.

"Is there any sign of a problem elsewhere?" Ward asked.

"Not yet. I've ordered the entire GD-3 program shut down."

"God, who would have thought," said Ward, turning to address the reader. "All we wanted was a bigger, healthier tomato."

Jim Richardson, the Press Secretary, walked away from the sheriff and rejoined Larry and Ward. "The sheriff tells me there were reports of incidents all over the county."

"Oh, that's balderdash and poppycock," said Larry. "One nut spots a flying saucer, and pretty soon everybody is shaking hands with little green men."

"You mean there's an alien invasion going on, too?" asked Ward. Then he cringed, waiting for Larry to call him a wiener again.

Jim glared at Larry. "The problem with your skepticism is that there are tomatoes attacking us as we speak. Look at that soldier. He's about to shoot some of them. See? He just killed one. So when we're in the midst of a tomato attack, your comment about everybody shaking hands with little green men, while pithy, doesn't really correlate."

Larry glared at Ward. "I see that the soldier killed the tomato with a bullet, even though you said bullets were useless against them. I think you owe bullets an apology."

Ward glared at Larry. "No, I said that bullets worked fine. The tomatoes were just hard to hit."

"Oh. Well, I'll be honest. I only process about a third of what you say."

The soldier killed another tomato and smiled, very proud of his accomplishment.

"Maybe the tomato menace *has* been contained," said Jim.

"Maybe it has," said Ward. "Doesn't make much of an end-of-the-chapter cliffhanger, though."

"It does if the reader recognizes the irony."

"That's true."

"Maybe the tomato menace *has* been contained," said Jim.

CHAPTER 3

The Pentagon (Washington, D.C.)

They couldn't pretend the tomato problem didn't exist. Well, they *could*, and some in the media got rich doing just that. But a group of high-ranking-but-obscure military officials, scientists, and politicians waited in the hallway to discuss solutions.

"Where'd you get this one, General?" asked a politician, pointing to one of the general's medals.

"Oh, I won that in a three-legged sack race, last Armed Forces Day picnic."

"And that one?"

"Woolworth. It covers a rip in my shirt."

"And that one?"

"Gallantry in action during World War II."

Major Millis arrived. "Sorry I'm late, gentlemen," he said, not sounding very sorry at all, and in fact a bit proud of his tardiness. "Would you follow me, please?"

He led them to their luxurious meeting room. A long fancy table was surrounded by comfortable leather chairs with plenty of room between them. The generals, scientists, and politicians all made satisfied "*Ahhhh*" sounds as they sat down. Everybody was happy.

"Now, are we all here?" asked Major Millis.

Everybody in the room indicated that they were, in fact, there.

A general raised his hand. "Are there to be doughnuts?"

"Are there to be doughnuts?" repeated Major Millis, with a great big smile on his face. "You'd better believe it!"

[*Editor's Note*: Where else would his smile be, on his belly? Overly wordy. Please be more concise.]

[*Author's Note*: Wow. Talk about being a pedantic.]

[*Editor's Note*: Pedant.]

[*Author's Note*: Maybe his smile *was* on his belly. This is the kind of wacky novelization where somebody's belly button could be smiling. I've got the giggles just thinking about it.]

[*Editor's Note*: That crosses a little too far into surrealism. Let's keep things grounded. If we lose our readers' suspension of disbelief, they'll switch to a real book.]

[*Author's Note*: These comments are covering up a hilarious and viciously satirical sequence where all of these high-ranking people are debating the kind of doughnuts they want. Thanks a lot.]

[*Editor's Note*: Well, excuuuuuuuuuse me!]

"I'm glad everybody is finally happy with their doughnuts," said Major Millis. "Now that we're all here, I'd like to turn the meeting over to Dr. Morrison."

Dr. Morrison stood. "As I'm sure you're aware, this tomato problem has caused considerable concern within the scientific community."

"I wasn't aware of that," said a man sitting near the back. "So I thank you for the information."

"Scientists throughout the nation have directed their attention to this very vexing—and I do mean *vexing*—goodness gracious is it ever vexing—issue with only limited success. Brows are furrowed in every laboratory. However, with the help of Dr. Fuji Nokitofa, we believe we've made a breakthrough. Gentlemen, may I present Dr. Fuji Nokitofa."

Dr. Nokitofa stood and nodded politely. He'd been told there'd be applause, but didn't let the lack of it distract him.

"How do you do, Doctor?" asked Dr. Morrison.

"Very well, thank you," said Dr. Nokitofa in a poorly dubbed voice. (We are forced to acknowledge that this joke doesn't translate very well to the printed page, but with a little imagination on the part of you, the reader, it's actually quite clever.)

"Dr. Nokitofa, would you please explain the project to the gentlemen?"

"Yes," said Dr. Nokitofa, still badly dubbed. "That is why I am here, and it is why you introduced me just now, and I almost certainly would have taken the initiative to explain the project without being prompt-ed." He cleared his poorly dubbed throat. "What we have developed is, in essence, a half-man, half-robot."

"My God!" said a general. "That idea is so crazy it just might work!"

"人間の知性と超人的な力の非常に洗練された組み合わせ。"

"Wait, wait," said Dr. Morrison. "Dubbed into English, please."

"My apologies. I said, a very sophisticated combination of human intelligence and superhuman powers."

"My God!" said the general. "This just keeps getting crazier and crazier! It will definitely work!"

"We are confident that this will result in the complete destruction of the enemy," said Dr. Nokitofa.

"Are there any comments, gentlemen?" asked Major Millis.

Mr. Black stood up, having plenty of room to do so. "As head of the Federal Intelligence Agency, I certainly don't mean to question the background of these fine gentlemen, but frankly, I don't think the answer to this problem lies in trinkets and gadgets."

"It's not a trinket," said Dr. Morrison. "It's a $200 million cyborg that's already been built and is ready to eliminate the tomato menace with the push of a button."

"$200 million? We could've had almost thirty-four six-million-dollar men for that!"

"Right. But what's spent is spent. I'm literally saying that there's an on/off switch currently set to 'off' that could easily be set to 'on' and solve our problem."

Mr. Black angrily shook his head. "No robots! This is man versus vegetable!"

"Technically," said Dr. Nokitofa, "tomatoes are fags."

Everybody fell into an uncomfortable silence.

"He means fruits," Dr. Morrison clarified.

The uncomfortable silence lingered.

Major Millis forced a smile. "Right. Fruits. Hey, it's 1978 and we can all enjoy that, right? Product of our time. Nobody's feelings are hurt. We've got another decade or so, easily, where it's just jolly good harmless fun. After that, we might want to phase it out. But for now, fruits indeed!"

"Anyway," said Dr. Morrison, "the robot—"

"Enough with the robot," said Major Millis. "Nobody wants to hear about your precious robot. Read the room, man!"

"バイト-ミー."

"Watch your tone, Dr. Nokitofa. Even un-dubbed, we get the gist."

"My apologies. I shall bask in shame now."

"Gentlemen," said Major Millis. "Allow me to introduce Mason Dixon."

"Like the line?" Dr. Morrison asked.

"What line? Mason Dixon is confusingly important to our efforts to stop the tomatoes, and I've been authorized to assign him four of my best agents. Gentlemen, with your permission, I'd like to introduce Mr. Dixon to his operatives."

"Hypothetically," asked one of the generals, "what would happen if we didn't give that permission?"

"That honestly hadn't occurred to me," said Major Millis. "I saw no reason you'd withhold it."

"Then why did you ask? It sounds to me like somebody is trying to pad out the word count in a book."

"Nonsense! The 'with your permission' line came directly from the movie. There's no conspiracy here. If anything, the padding came from your dialogue, not mine."

"That's fair," said the general. "Permission granted."

"Despite some minor recruitment difficulties caused by our recent PR problems," said Major Millis, "I believe you'll find that your unit will meet the highest of standards."

"What PR problems?" asked Mason.

"You know, all the tomato-related deaths. And the widespread, shameless corruption."

They walked into a room where Mason's team awaited. The first was a black man with a very large Caucasian nose. Mason stared at him, wondering how this had happened. Had he lost his nose in an accident, and a white man's nose was surgically attached to his face? Was he born to parents of two different races, and all of the white parent's genes had gone to his nose? So many questions.

"Sam Smith," said Major Millis. "Disguise expert."

Ooohhhhh! If you looked very closely, yes, he was in fact wearing a pair of glasses that were attached to a false nose. The illusion was remarkable.

The next member of the team was a woman wearing several gold medals.

"Gretta Attenbaum, swimming expert," said Major Millis. "Gretta defected to us after the last Olympics. We feel that she'll be quite an addition to the department."

"Right," said Mason. "I have to admit that I'm a little baffled by why a swimming expert is going to help us defeat the tomatoes."

"Oh, there's more bafflement in store. Here's the next member of your team: Greg Colburn, underwater expert." He pointed to a man in full scuba diving gear.

"Yeah, I noticed him as soon as we walked in the room," said Mason. "So two-thirds of the team you've introduced so far has an aquatic specialty."

Major Millis frowned. "Hmmm. The redundancy

hadn't occurred to me until now. Oh well. Too late now."

"You said I'd be introduced to four operatives," said Mason. "I only see three. Is the fourth one...invisible?"

"The Operative Room is no place for silliness," said Major Millis. "Of course he's not invisible. He's simply not here. Lieutenant Finletter is winding up his current mission."

"Was the actor playing him unavailable?"

"No."

"It's okay if he wasn't. We all have day jobs here."

"No! He'll contact you at these coordinates," said Major Millis, handing Mason a paper with some coordinates on it. "Expect him at ten-hundred hours. And don't try saying 'Ten hundred hours? I can't wait that long!' It's ten o'clock a.m. and you darn well know it."

"I'm not prone to tomfoolery," said Mason. "I'll be there." He looked at his team. "But may God help us all."

"God couldn't make it. Sorry."

CHAPTER 4

The Ocean (Pacific.)

The ocean hides many dangers within its dark waters. Giant squid, capable of crushing a submarine in their sucker-laden tentacles. Great white sharks, known for closing beaches and destroying the economies of small towns. Blue whales, the world's largest mammal, so cruel that they would devour a living puppet whole. Crabs, whose succulent insides are covered by lots of spiky parts that could poke you. Water-breathing death monkeys, the fiercest primate of them all, capable of ripping an adult human male's arms clean off, leaving him defenseless against an approaching great white shark.

Yet the ocean can also be peaceful. A place for bikini-wearing teenagers who want only to lie in the sun and discuss the issues of the day. A place where a young boy could sit on a boat and gaze upon those bikini-wearing teenagers, thinking impure yet understandable thoughts. A place where youths could frolic in the water, splashing away happily, getting in a cardiovascular workout without a care in the world.

On this day, the ocean was not peaceful.

Because as the youths swam, a giant squid made its way toward them, hungry for prey.

It sliced through the water like an arrow, possibly because of its arrow-shaped head. It was forty feet long, including its tentacles, which was not a world record but very close. Death was headed for these swimming youth, and none of them saw it coming.

But Little Timmy saw it. Not the Little Timmy who'd been eaten earlier—a different Little Timmy. He saw the shadow of the beast heading toward the swimmers. He quickly looked around for a harpoon, but his catamaran was not equipped with one.

"*Squid!*" he shouted.

Less than a hundred feet separated the giant squid from the swimmers. There was no possibility of them swimming to shore in time. Their young lives were about to be extinguished in their prime. None of them would achieve their goals. Yes, they would probably become famous for getting killed by a giant squid, but that would be little consolation as their crushed bodies bobbed along the surface of the water.

The squid continued to swim toward them. So hungry. An eternal hunger that could never truly be sated.

The squid, however, had not anticipated the tomatoes.

Hundreds of them floated in the water.

Had they been waiting for a giant squid to swim over to them? Probably not. It's impossible to say, since the minds of killer tomatoes remain a mystery. But they knew an opportunity when they saw it, or sensed it, or whatever the hell they did, and this squid looked like quite the feast.

The squid saw the tomatoes and scoffed. Tomatoes! The most harmless of vegetables!

The tomatoes converged, forming a barricade between the squid and its human meal. The squid scoffed again. Did the foolish beings truly believe that they could stop it? The giant squid would smash through those tomatoes like an octopus smashing through Brussels sprouts.

But when it struck the tomatoes, the squid felt something it had not experienced in a long, long time. Pain.

The tomatoes began to speak. The squid could not understand their language, but their underwater babbling was clearly mockery.

The squid would not be mocked.

It lashed out with six of its ten mighty tentacles. Dozens of tomatoes split wide open upon impact, their slimy innards mixing with the salt water. The squid lashed out again with the remaining four, sending dozens more tomatoes to their watery graves.

But the other tomatoes did not flee. If anything, they floated toward the squid with renewed purpose.

The squid killed more and more of them. But for every tomato it destroyed, two more took its place. They seemed infinite! The squid knew nothing of what constituted a reasonable number of tomatoes, but this seemed like a lot.

Its tentacles lashed with more vigor. Yet this vigor was borne of panic. The squid was beginning to realize that, impossibly, it might lose this battle.

Finally, the squid tried to turn around. It would swim back to its underwater kingdom and dine upon dolphins or clownfish instead.

Alas, no. The tomatoes were having none of that. They surrounded the squid, babbling with maniacal intent, set on destroying this behemoth. Oh, it fought back mightily, yet no amount of tentacle thrashing could defeat the combined force of the killer tomatoes. And soon the giant squid had used its gills to diffuse oxygen from the water into its blood for the last time.

The swimming youths had been so transfixed by the sight of tomatoes battling a giant squid that they'd forgotten that they were in danger.

"Run!" shouted Little Timmy. He obviously meant "Swim!" but anybody could have made that mistake in the heat of the moment.

The youths tried their best, but their foolish decision to have fun in the water would be their demise. Tomatoes floated everywhere. So much screaming. So much splashing. So much flailing. So much...

...dying.

Little Timmy watched it all from his catamaran. At least it wasn't—no, wait, it was sinking. He was doomed. Not a single bikini top had been eaten away by a tomato, so he didn't even have that to bring joy to his final moments. One would like to report that he perished bravely, but Little Timmy's death was cowardly and quite frankly more than a little embarrassing.

The tomatoes floated in the water. Sated. For now.

But only for now.

CHAPTER 5

White House Press Briefing Room (Des Moines, Iowa.)

Press Secretary Jim Richardson thought this briefing was going remarkably well. The press had been grilling him about inflation, the gas shortage, foreign relations, and the president putting an unreasonable burden upon the taxpayers with his propensity for fluffy flower-print toilet paper. But nobody had asked about the tomatoes, and with only time for one more question, Jim was confident that he'd make it through this press conference unscathed.

Several hands went up, but the best part of being Press Secretary was that *he* got to choose who to call on. The power was intoxicating.

An adorable little girl sat near the back, representing *Puppies & Ponies* magazine. She wasn't a legitimate journalist; she'd won a "Be a Reporter at a White House Press Briefing" contest. Her prize-winning essay was about who would win in a fight: a puppy or a pony.

She'd definitely lob a softball question his way.

Jim pointed at her. "You. Little girl."

"Barbara Jenks, sir," she said. "*Puppies & Ponies.* I have a question, sir."

"And I'm sure it's a sweet, innocent question, just like you. What would you like to know?"

"We've heard nothing at all about the growing tomato menace."

Jim froze. Blast! He could never have imagined that his choice of question-askers could backfire like this!

All of the reporters in the room sat at attention, pens hovered over their notebooks in anticipation. This was going to be far more interesting than his fourteen-minute answer about the toilet paper scandal.

"I…" said Jim.

"Uh…" said Jim.

"I…" said Jim.

"Er…" said Jim.

What was he going to do? He couldn't *fib* at a White House press briefing! Such a thing was unheard of! This was the room where honesty reigned supreme. The last bastion of candor and transparency. He couldn't stretch the truth! Not here!

Or could he…?

It had never been tried before. All White House press secretaries before and after would shake their heads with disapproval at such behavior. But maybe Jim could—he couldn't believe he was even considering this—downplay the threat. He wouldn't actually make an untrue statement; he'd simply massage reality a bit.

Jim forced a smile. "I wouldn't exactly call it a menace, young lady. There have been some isolated reports…"

He was beginning to perspire.

"...alleged incidents involving some unusual activity..."

His stomach hurt.

"...associated with this, uh, particular vegetable..."

Jim prayed that he wouldn't throw up all over the podium. The reporters would probably include that detail in their stories.

"...but I assure you that, uh, uh, uh, this is not and never will become a menace, by my own personal definition of menace."

He was getting dizzy. The world was turning black, but he'd almost made it through this. Only a few more seconds of mild dishonesty and it would all be over.

"However, our wise and trustworthy president, leaving no stone unturned, has called upon our most noted congressional leaders in this field, of which there are many, to begin a thorough, intensive, painstaking..."

Jim took out his pocket thesaurus.

"...and exhaustive investigation into the backgrounds and origins of this...interesting quirk of nature."

He shook the sweat off his body like a dog after a bath.

"Furthermore, you can assure your young readers that this will never become a problem that Americans need fear."

He'd done it. He'd gotten through it.

"Did that answer your question?" he asked.

Barbara finished writing in her notebook. "So you're saying that there is no problem?"

Jim nodded. "Yes. Yes, that's what I'm saying."

"Despite reports of people being eaten by tomatoes all across the country?"

Jim chuckled. "I think you're misreading them.

There are reports of people eating tomatoes all across the country. And who among us doesn't enjoy a nice BLT? I could go for one right now."

"Why would there be nationwide reports about people eating tomatoes?" asked Barbara. "That's not newsworthy. It becomes newsworthy when the BLTs are eating people."

"Look, you ill-bred little brat!" Jim shouted. "I don't appreciate being contradicted in front of all these nice people who are simply trying to write stories for their newspapers. Are you trying to confuse them?"

"I just want the truth."

"There is no tomato menace," said Jim. "There is no tomato menace...there is no tomato menace..."

"Excuse me," said a reporter in the front row. "Are you trying to hypnotize that little girl?"

"Of course not."

"That's kind of the vibe I got from the way you were modulating your voice and waving your hands."

"Enough of your wretched insolence! I will not be questioned! Out! Everybody out!"

United States Capitol Building (Toronto, Ontario.)

"This meeting of the senate subcommittee on Domestic Tomato Growth and Expansion is called to order," said Senator Wayne, banging his gavel. "Does everybody have a copy of the report?"

"I don't," said Senator Alfred.

"That's odd. I'm sometimes shaky on the larger numbers, but five has never eluded me before. I wonder what happened to the fifth copy? Oh well. I'm sure it didn't fall into the wrong hands."

"I have my copy," said Senator Charles. "And someday I might read it, but *today is not that day*. My constituents don't like hearing about unpleasant things, so I will be proposing the 'head in the sand' course of action."

Senator Wayne nodded. "All in favor of heads in the sand?"

"Actually," said Senator Frank, "the situation is becoming rather dire, and—"

Senator Wayne pounded his gavel. "The ayes have it."

"But—"

"I said, the ayes have it."

————

Conrad Whitpool, editor-in-chief of the Daily Herald, was not as mean as J. Jonah Jameson at the Daily Bugle, but Conrad had the edge in that he was not a fictional character. His fists had pounded on his desk so many times that there were indentations all over it, causing him to frequently spill his coffee on the uneven surface.

On his desk, not yet covered with coffee, was a copy of the Senate Subcommittee on Domestic Tomato Growth and Expansion report. Yes, the very copy that Senator Alfred didn't have in the last section. The pieces are all coming together now, aren't they? Though some critics would like to call the construction of this story "haphazard at best," perhaps things aren't as random as they seem...

The government was trying to hide the tomato story from the general public, but Conrad's whole deal was sharing stories with the general public that the government was trying to hide. The inside of the report was stamped *"Do not share with the lying jerks in the media,"* but that wouldn't stop him.

"Julius!" he shouted.

His assistant, Julius, walked to the doorway, spent a few moments working up his courage, and then stepped into Conrad's office, trembling.

"Get me Goldstein," said Conrad.

"He's still in Beirut, sir."

"Business or pleasure?"

"I—"

"Never mind. Get me Johnson."

"He's covering that trial in Texas."

"The good one or the bad one?"

"I—"

"Never mind." Conrad pounded on his desk. "Who *is* available?"

"Well," said Julius, "there's you, sir."

"Me?"

"It's never too late to learn a new skill, sir. Instead of correcting our mistakes, you could make mistakes of your own."

Conrad beat the crap out of Julius. When he was done, they resumed their conversation.

"Wait a minute," said Julius. "There's Fairchild."

"Who the hell is he?"

"She, sir. Lois Fairchild. The new kid. Society section."

"Aw, cripes. Dames have no place in journalism. They're too concerned with their penmanship. All those fancy little curls on the letters."

"She's the only one available."

"All right, all right. Send her in."

Lois Fairchild nervously walked toward the editor-in-chief's office. What could he possibly want?

Was he going to yell at her? Shout at her? Holler at her? All three?

She gently rapped on his open door. "Fairchild, sir."

"Hmmm?"

"You sent for me."

"Did I?" Conrad frowned. "Sorry. I lost my short-term memory in a novelty exploding cigar incident. Haven't been able to enjoy a cigar since. I'll light one up and instead of savoring the soothing flavor I spend the whole time waiting for it to blow up in my face. It's no way to live, Fairchild. No way to live."

"Is that why you called me here?"

"The cigar stuff? Cripes, I hope not. That would be a waste of your time, and more importantly, mine."

"Okay," said Lois.

They stared at each other for a moment.

"Have a seat," said Conrad.

Lois nervously sat down.

"Fairchild, I've been keeping my eye on you. You've got a good sense of organization."

"Thank you, sir."

"Fluid style."

"Thank you, sir."

"Sharp mind."

"Thank you, sir."

"A nice ass."

Lois said nothing.

Conrad chuckled. "Accept the compliment, Fairchild. That's the way male bosses get to talk to their female employees, and I'm confident that nobody in future generations will ever call us out on our poor behavior. Anyway, I'm about to give you a challenge. Your first big assignment."

"Technically, sir, my expose last month brought down the entire—"

"Yep, your first big assignment. And I expect you to use every attribute at your disposal. You understand what I mean by that, right? I don't want to have to explain it in graphic and misogynistic detail, but I will. What I'm saying is that you're a woman, and most people in positions of power are men, and there are ways that women who look like you can encourage men in positions of power to...look, you know how sex works, right?"

"Yes, sir."

"Good." He slid the senate committee report across the desk. "This will give you the necessary background to handle the assignment. Go to it."

"Right away, sir," said Lois.

"One more thing, Fairchild. I'm certain the government will go to unbelievable lengths to ensure the secrecy of this thing. What I'm saying is that I'm putting you in danger. A lot of danger. More danger than any new reporter from the Society section should have to endure. If you're captured and tortured, the Daily Herald and I will disavow all knowledge of your existence. Got it?"

"Got it, sir."

Lois Fairchild strode out of the editor-in-chief's office. The world might not know the truth about the killer tomatoes yet, but it would. Oh, yes. It would.

CHAPTER 6

A day at the motorcycle races was fun for the entire family. You could see fast-moving cycles, crazy stunts, and maybe even a broken leg or two!

Rick raced down the dirt hill, imagining that he was Evel Knievel, the fanciest cyclist of them all. The pretty girls cheered as he sped past the checkpoint, but he only cared about one of them. His best girl, Petunia. They were going to be married someday. Because of his high-speed live-for-the-moment lifestyle, he and Petunia had discussed that he was certain to die in a tragic motorcycle accident, leaving her a young widow, but she was okay with that as long as they kissed a lot before his death.

There she was, looking gorgeous in her late 1970's fashion.

Rick winked, which she couldn't see because of his goggles, and blew her a kiss, which she couldn't see because he'd already passed her.

Blowing her a kiss had been a mistake. One of the most important rules of motorcycle safety, right after "Don't ride into quicksand," was to keep both hands on the hand grips at all times.

Rick's motorcycle fell to the ground, tumbling him out onto the fluffy dirt.

He did a routine check to see if he'd broken any bones. He hadn't. Disappointed, he started to get up, but then he noticed the tomato lying on the ground next to him.

You didn't often find tomatoes lying around on dirt motorcycle racing tracks. Rick picked it up. Maybe he'd put it in a salad tonight.

Petunia was hurrying over to him, a look of concern on her face. He was confused by her concern, then remembered the motorcycle accident he'd had a few seconds ago.

"Look!" he said. "A funky little tomato!"

Then Rick winced in pain.

He gazed at his hand in horror. He'd previously had five fingers—he'd counted them before the race—and now he had only three.

Surely the tomato hadn't eaten two of his fingers! Had he lost them in the accident and simply not noticed? That was far-fetched, but not as far-fetched as having them bitten off by a tomato!

Suddenly there was more pain. Now his hand was down to two fingers. (If you counted his thumb as a finger, which Rick did.)

"What madness is this?" he wailed.

This time he watched the tomato closely. It bit off his last two fingers.

He had no more fingers on his hand! Did it even count as a hand anymore?

With no fingers to hold the tomato, it slipped out of his grasp and fell to the ground.

"Rick!" Petunia screamed. "What happened to your fingers?"

Rick tried to point at the tomato but couldn't.

"The tomato!" Rick shouted. "It was the tomato!"

"Calm down," said Petunia. "I know you're all out of sorts from your disfigurement, but you can't go blaming a tomato. It makes you sound like a crazy person."

"I'm not crazy!" Rick insisted. "The tomato did it!"

Petunia whirled her index finger around her ear, a gesture that Rick could not duplicate. "You lost them in a grisly motorcycle accident," she said. "You need to accept that so you can move on. Not with your motorcycle riding, of course, but with a less fulfilling life." She glanced around at the ground. "Now where are they?"

"They're in its tummy!" Rick screamed.

"Don't be ridiculous. Tomatoes don't have tummies. Seriously, Rick, we need to find your fingers so they can sew them back on. All of this tomato-blaming is wasting valuable time. Fingers start to get moldy not long after they're severed, so we don't have time to waste. We need to find your fingers, put them in the ice we're using to keep the beer cold, get you to a hospital, ask if they're the kind of hospital that provides finger re-attachment services, make sure they take your insurance, and then let the doctors sew your fingers back on. They probably won't bend or do much but flop around after that, but at least you won't have a fingerless hand!"

"It was the tomato!" Rick bellowed, trying to stomp on the finger-eating monster.

"Sweetheart, you're scaring me," said Petunia. "That tomato did not eat your fingers. Look how timid it is. Look at the way it..."

Petunia's jaw dropped open as the realization hit her. The tomato had rolled out of the way to avoid being stomped on.

Not possible. Maybe it was gravity.

Rick stomped again, and the tomato rolled out of

the way. The tomato was alive! Well, technically all tomatoes were alive, but this tomato was alive enough to roll out of the way of a stomping foot!

Petunia screamed.

Rick slammed his foot down again, this time smashing the tomato into the dirt. It split open, oozing seeds and tomato gook. Rick crouched down and began to frantically sift through the slime for his fingers.

Petunia screamed again.

"There's no need to be afraid any longer," said Rick. "It's dead."

"I'm not afraid of that particular tomato!" said Petunia. "But look! Look!"

Hundreds of tomatoes rolled down the dirt hill.

Petunia stared at them in horror. "We can't defeat this many of them!"

"Not alone, we can't," said Rick.

"Our love won't get us through this!"

"That's not what I meant. When a bunch of motorcycle racers and the girls cheering them on team up, there's nothing they can't do!"

All of the motorcyclists drove up behind Rick and Petunia, followed by the girls who'd been cheering them on. The tomatoes continued to roll down the hill, babbling in their eerie language, getting closer and closer.

"Kill the tomatoes!" shouted a girl, dropping the starter flag.

The motorcyclists sped toward their enemy. Dozens of tomatoes burst under their tires.

Rick raised his fingerless fist into the air. "Yes! We're winning!"

The riders spun around in circles, smearing tomatoes all over the dirt. Some of them popped wheelies, the spinning tires coming down on tomatoes and spraying their tomato guts high into the air.

In the battle of man versus vegetable, man was winning.

But with an early victory comes hubris. And the motorcyclists, seeing how easily their vehicles splattered the enemy, began to show off. It was no longer enough to simply pop a wheelie onto a tomato; no, they had to use the ramps to jump high into the air. And as the racetrack became littered with the corpses of hundreds of tomatoes, the riders' overconfidence grew and grew.

The remaining tomatoes formed themselves into a pyramid. An onlooker conducting an objective assessment of the situation would conclude that, despite the many recent victories the cyclists had won over the tomatoes, driving into the tomato pyramid would not be a wise idea. Even you, the reader, forced to rely upon a mental picture, have enough information to figure out that you shouldn't try to plow your motorcycle into that thing.

The cyclists, meanwhile, came to a very different conclusion. They thought it would be a *splendid* idea to crash into the tomato pyramid. Why, they'd be killing the rest of the tomatoes in one fell swoop!

But, like a free lunch, there is no such thing as one fell swoop.

It doesn't matter which of the cyclists drove into the tomato pyramid first—with his helmet and goggles you couldn't really see his face anyway. When he struck the pyramid, he no doubt expected tomatoes to go flying everywhere. But they did not. They held firm.

To be clear, not every single tomato survived the impact. The ones who got hit directly by the front tire of the motorcycle didn't fare very well. But the overwhelming majority of the tomatoes were not mangled by the tire, and as the anonymous rider came to a more abrupt stop than he'd expected, he realized that he'd made quite a blunder.

The cyclists and the pretty girls watched as the rider disappeared into the tomatoes.

Instead of learning from his poor choice, the other cyclists revved their engines and sped toward the tomatoes. One by one they smacked into the pyramid, which was now more of a "pile," and one by one their now-riderless motorcycles came out the other side.

"Run!" Petunia screamed. She grabbed Rick's hand, but it was fingerless and slippery, and she wasn't able to hold on. The other pretty girls also screamed as the tomatoes left their pile and rolled toward them. The tomatoes hurled themselves into the air, taking down pretty girl after pretty girl.

All they'd wanted was to watch a motorcycle race. And it cost them their lives. The story of the attack of the killer tomatoes, though filled with lighthearted political satire, is also a heartbreaking cautionary tale.

Petunia and Rick were the only two left. And they were completely surrounded by the tomatoes.

"Our love will protect us!" Rick promised.

"Will it, though?" asked Petunia.

"Feel it! Feel the love thumping away in your heart! No tomato in the world can take it away from us!"

"Okay, so you're taking more of an abstract view here. You're not actually saying that our love is going to *stop* us from dying; you're saying that we'll die in love, which is better than not dying in love."

"Exactly," said Rick. "Our love will distract us, but we're boned."

And the young lovers were indeed boned. They fought mightily side by side, until the tomatoes ate

Rick, after which Petunia fought mightily by herself. But soon, Petunia also fell, and in her final moments she took solace in the knowledge that someday she and Chad would be reunited. (Chad was two boyfriends ago, and she'd always regretted breaking up with him. He was alive and well right now, but he couldn't stay that way forever, and she longed for their ghostly embrace.)

CHAPTER 7

Larry and Ward drove toward the racing track, siren blaring.

Nobody expects you to remember every character in this epic cast. Most likely, you're setting the book aside for a couple of weeks after each chapter, to savor the experience. C'mon, you don't want to burn through *Attack of the Killer Tomatoes* in a few hours. What would you do then? Read other books? Spend time with the elderly? Dance?

Anyway, you may have forgotten who Larry and Ward are, and any other book would expect you to flip back through the pages to refresh your memory, or ask the narrator of the audiobook version to repeat himself. But not this book. Though it may not always seem like it, I know your time is valuable, and I am pleased to provide you with this helpful reminder.

Larry and Ward work for the Department of Agriculture. They were in that awesome scene where the helicopter crashed. The one that was an actual helicopter crash on the set of the movie. Can you imagine if somebody had died making *Attack of the Killer Tomatoes?* Hard to even imagine.

Right?

Hard to even imagine.

I promise I'll get back to the story soon. It's just that something's been weighing on my mind, and it's the reason the last couple of chapters haven't been as well-written as what came before.

What's a major theme of *Attack of the Killer Tomatoes?*

The anguish of loss? Yes, I suppose so, but that's not the one I mean.

If God is kind and just, why would He allow these tomatoes to attack people? Again, yes, that is an important theme, but it's not where I'm trying to lead you.

Hiding the truth.

This is a story about hiding the truth from the public.

Let me ask you: Why were the filmmakers spending so much time mulling over the theme of hiding the truth? Do you think anybody went into that movie theater seeking a thematic exploration of hiding the truth? No. They wanted to see tomatoes killing people. And maybe enjoy a few rousing musical numbers. And perhaps some nudity, though they left disappointed.

I think you know where I'm going with this. You saw that helicopter crash. It's right there in the movie. Nobody could have survived that. The filmmakers are all like "Oh, ho, ho, it was jolly fun because nobody got badly hurt!" Yet doesn't it seem suspicious that they then proceeded to make a movie about hiding the truth from the public?

Why was that theme on their minds?

What subconscious guilt might the filmmakers have been harboring that manifested itself in their work?

I'm not saying that the passengers died in that helicopter crash. I'm *alleging* that they did, which is an important distinction from a legal perspective.

I'm also not asking for the filmmakers to be punished. They brought a lot of joy to the world with their creation, and for that deserve immunity for their crime. All I'm asking is…honestly, I don't know what I'm asking. I just needed to get that off of my chest. I considered not finishing the novelization, but the contract has been signed, the check has been cashed, and the yacht has been bought, so I have no choice.

Don't worry about me. I'll be fine. Gonna take a few pills and forget about this for a while.

———

Hey, welcome back to *Attack of the Killer Tomatoes: The Movie That You Read.*

Anyway, Larry and Ward work for the Department of Agriculture. Larry's the one who shouts a lot. Ward is the other one. They were speeding toward the racing track, siren blaring. Why did guys from the Department of Agriculture have a siren on their car? I dunno. Maybe they just do. I've never met anybody from the Department of Agriculture.

"Where are we going?" asked Ward, holding on for dear life. He couldn't count on his seatbelt to protect him if they crashed—it was 1978 and nobody wore them.

"A bunch of bikers and their fans got munched on by a herd of tomatoes," said Larry.

"Is a group of tomatoes called a herd?" asked Ward. "I thought it was called a grumble."

"You're thinking of pugs."

"Oh, right. A grumble of pugs." Ward smiled at

the mental image that conveyed. "Actually, a group of tomatoes is called a clutch."

"Are you more afraid of a clutch of tomatoes or a herd of tomatoes?" asked Larry.

"A herd."

"Then shut up."

"So what can we do?" asked Ward.

"We can keep it quiet, that's what."

"Didn't you hear the radio? It's solid tomatoes between here and Holtville. We're liable to get killed."

"Will you can it, you little pud-puller?" asked Larry. "If John Q. Public finds out what's really going down, we're as good as dead."

"Are you calling me little, the pud I'm pulling little, or both?"

"It doesn't matter."

"It matters to me."

They arrived at the racetrack. Ward's first thought was that it didn't look so bad, but then he noticed the dead bodies strewn everywhere. There were a lot of smashed tomatoes. Those brave motorcyclists and the brave pretty girls who'd been cheering them on had put up quite a fight.

"Maybe they defeated them," said Larry.

"Is that good or bad?" asked Ward.

"What do you mean, is that good or bad? It's good, you little udder-yanker!"

"I don't like the way you speak to me. You're always trying to be demeaning and hurtful. Did it ever occur to you that the reason I'm so bad at my job is because there's never any positive reinforcement? What's wrong with 'Atta boy, Ward, that's the best observation I've heard all day!' or 'Atta boy, Ward, those sideburns are spectacular!'? You break me down instead of building me up."

For a moment, Larry looked genuinely apologetic. But then he glanced out the windshield. "Look out there!"

"A grumble of pugs?"

"No, you melon-squeezer! Tomatoes! A clutch of tomatoes!"

Ward could never have imagined that so many tomatoes could gather in one place. There were literally hundreds of them and figuratively millions of them. And they were all rolling right at the car!

"We're going to die!" Ward screamed, cynically.

Within moments, the car was covered in tomatoes. Larry put the car in reverse and floored the gas pedal. Driving at full speed backwards on a curvy dirt road in a vehicle covered by tomatoes worked for a while, until they crashed.

Larry desperately grabbed the radio speaker. "Do you read me? Do you read me?" he asked, sounding like an unloved book.

"Are you happy now?" Ward shouted at him. "You kept it so secret, nobody knows where we are?"

"No, I'm not happy!" Larry shouted back. "Do I *look* happy? Am I smiling? Am I singing?"

"Maybe you're smiling and singing on the inside!"

"Do you read? Do you read?" he shouted into the radio speaker, sounding like an author at a poorly attended book signing.

Ward yanked the speaker out of his hand. "Help me! S.O.S.! S.O.S.!"

"Give me that!"

"O.M.G.! W.T.F.!"

"I said, give me that!"

"You can't tell me to shut up! I quit!"

"I didn't tell you to shut up!"

"You did earlier!"

"You can't quit!" said Larry. "The department—"

"Screw the department! I'm gonna die!"

"I'm gonna die, too!"

"Good!"

Larry frowned. "You don't really mean that, do you?"

The back windshield shattered.

"No," said Ward. "I don't. Let's not die like this. Arguing."

Tomatoes poured into the car by the dozens. Their babbling—their incessant, maddening babbling—was even louder when you were trapped in a car with them.

"Suicide pact?" asked Larry.

Ward nodded. "What are the terms?"

"I'll kill you, then you kill me."

"I'm not sure that will work."

More and more and more and more and more and more tomatoes poured into the car.

"I'll shoot you," said Larry, "and then you grab the gun really fast and shoot me back before you die."

"A bullet to the head would kill me instantly. I don't think I'd be able to return the favor."

"Then I'll shoot you in the chest."

"I wouldn't die from a chest wound before the tomatoes got me. I'd essentially be in agony from getting shot in the chest while the tomatoes gobbled me up. It would defeat the whole purpose."

"Well, excuse me, Mr. Expert On Suicide Pacts!"

"Do you even have a gun?" Ward asked.

"I assumed that you did."

"If I had a gun, I'd be shooting tomatoes right now!"

"Fair enough," said Larry. "What if we, I don't know, smashed each other's faces into the gearshift?"

"That would work if we weren't already engulfed." Ward gestured, calling attention to the fact that the entire front of the car was now filled with carnivorous vegetables. "Die well, Larry."

"Die well, you wiener."

CHAPTER 8

The Oval Office (The White House.) (1600 Pennsylvania Avenue NW, Washington D.C. 20500.)

Press Secretary Jim Richardson sat across from the president's desk. The President of the United States of America, Wilbur Griffin in this part of the multiverse, shoved another pistachio into his mouth while he listened.

"Not good, Mr. President," said Jim. "Not good at all. Frankly, I was not overly impressed with the level of competency displayed by the scientific team."

"Do you know what *is* good?" asked President Griffin. "These pistachios. They're salty and delicious, but you don't have to struggle to open them the way you do a walnut. Get your thumbnails in there and they just pop right open, see?"

"Yes, Mr. President. It's a marvel of engineering."

"There's a lot we can learn from a pistachio, Jim."

"Such as, Mr. President?"

"Oh, sorry. I didn't think you'd ask me to elaborate. I'll get back to you on it. You were saying?"

"I haven't seen Dixon's special forces unit yet, but

if it's anything like what I've seen so far, I'd say we're in for a bit of trouble."

"Dixon?" asked President Griffin.

"Mason Dixon, Mr. President."

"Like the line?"

"What line?"

"Never mind. I think I've figured out what we can learn from a pistachio."

"Which is, sir?"

"If you squeeze them gently, it's like a little mouth. See that? I can make it open and close. I could do a funny voice, but that would be unbecoming of the President of the United States of America. Now, if I squeeze it too hard, the shell breaks open, but if you use the proper delicate touch, any pistachio can be a tiny talking mouth. Do you get the point I'm trying to make, Jim?"

"Not really, Mr. President."

"That breaks my heart, Jim. Breaks it right in two. Oh well. You were saying about the special forces?"

"I don't have much faith in them."

"I know what you mean," said President Griffin. "It's like trying to stack bibles on whipped cream. It's like trying to blow bubbles without gum or soap. It's like trying to train a pit bull when all you have is a Dachshund. It's like trying to swim across the Atlantic Ocean right after a heavy meal. It's like trying to perform open heart surgery on an unwilling patient. It's like trying to govern in a bipartisan manner. These are all very difficult things, Jim. Do you get my meaning, Jim?"

"I think so, Mr. President."

"You're not just saying that?"

"Not to the best of my knowledge, Mr. President."

"Jim, an unusual problem calls for an ingenious solution. And the people of this fine country awarded me 297 of the possible 538 electoral college votes because of my ability to come up with ingenious solutions. I think I've got one."

"I'm ready to listen, Mr. President."

"Are you sure? It won't go over your head, like my talking pistachios metaphor?"

"I'll try not to let it."

The president ate a few more pistachios, savoring each one in a way that made Jim mildly uncomfortable. "Have you ever heard of Mind Maker?"

"Certainly."

"Tell me what I already know, for the sake of exposition."

"It's the advertising agency you used in your campaign."

President Griffin nodded. "That's right. They said I'd never get re-elected. What did I do immediately after my first inauguration, Jim?"

"You lost the Statue of Liberty in a bar bet."

"You're damn right I did. And that made your job very difficult for a while, didn't it?"

"Yes, Mr. President. Extremely difficult."

"And did I redeem myself after that?"

"Not really, no."

"Exactly! And yet here I sit in the Oval Office, getting free snacks whenever I want on the taxpayer's dime, while my opponent is forced to make a fortune as a private citizen. Remember that time I got caught on a hot mike before my speech to those veterans?"

"Yes."

"So much profanity. So much blasphemy."

"I remember it well, Mr. President."

"The pundits thought my political career was over. But it wasn't. Some chalk my victory up to the American people having no sense of quality control. I say that it was because of Mind Maker."

"They did indeed work a miracle, Mr. President."

"I want you to fly to New York immediately. I want you to see Ted Swann. The man's a genius."

Jim nodded. "I'm on my way, Mr. President."

"And think about the pistachio thing. If you get really good, you can work two pistachios at once and make them have a silly conversation. Theoretically, you could even have them kiss, though I'm not there yet and maybe never will be."

"I'll think about it a lot, Mr. President."

A Grocery Store. (Anycity, USA.)

Manager Irving Dorkwobbler, who did not ascribe to the theory that funny names were a sign of desperation on the part of the writer, looked angrily at the bare spot in the produce section. He shouted for stock boy Eugene Waggawaggawagga to join him.

"Yes, sir?"

Irving gestured to the empty space. "What do you see here?"

"A dearth of tomatoes."

"Right. You're the stock boy, and your job is to keep them in stock. If tomatoes are suddenly selling like hotcakes, you should be constantly replenishing them."

"But there aren't any left in the back."

"Nonsense. We had plenty of them last time I checked."

"I know, but they aren't there now."

"What are you saying? They just rolled away on their own?"

"No, sir, I thought maybe somebody stole them."

"Who would steal a tomato?" asked Irving.

"Filmmakers?" asked Eugene.

"This mystery has to be solved as soon as possible. What if somebody comes into our store with the intention of purchasing a tomato, and there are no tomatoes to purchase? There'll be a shooting spree, that's what! We have to figure this out. Maybe a herd of tomatoes was misplaced."

"Sir!" said Eugene, pointing. "Did you see that?"

"You'll have to be more specific."

"The tomato rolling of its own accord!"

"That's what I thought you meant, but I wanted to be sure. Wow, look at the little fellow go!"

Suddenly it hit them: *the tomato was moving on its own.*

Another tomato rolled around the aisle. And then another. Followed by another. With another soon after that. And then yet another. And another. One more. One more after that. And another.

Irving and Eugene backed away. "Have you always treated the tomatoes with respect?" Irving whispered.

"I can't say that I have," Eugene admitted.

"Then we should run."

Irving and Eugene fled. Unfortunately, the tomatoes had already killed Jack Derpduhderpduh, who'd been mopping the floor when he met his fate. Irving and Eugene slipped on the wet floor, their arms pinwheeling in the air in unison as if they'd choreographed this beautiful ballet of death. They let out simultaneous "Ahhhh!"s, and then both of their heads struck the floor at the same time.

The tomatoes swarmed them.

———

What's it like to be eaten by a killer tomato?

It's not as bad as being eaten by a grizzly bear, but it's far worse than being eaten by a kitten.

In the unlikely event that you had to choose between being eaten by a killer tomato and eaten by a lion, you'd have a very difficult decision to make. Being eaten by a lion is more painful. They have those great big teeth and claws, and the entire process (I'm told) is extremely unpleasant. Yet there's a certain glory involved. "How did [*Your Name Here*] die?" "Eaten by a lion." "Whoa! That's badass!" There is nothing badass about being eaten by a tomato. Oh, your friends and family will try to pretend that there's dignity involved, but they're only fooling themselves.

If they love you, they'll say that you died in a skiing accident.

CHAPTER 9

Mason Dixon had spent all morning interviewing people about their tomato experiences. He grew more and more despondent after each one. There was simply no way to pretend that this story could be easily contained. Too many people had died. You could hardly throw a rock without hitting somebody who knew somebody who'd been killed by a tomato. Mason had verified this—three of the four rocks he threw hit people who knew somebody who'd been killed by a tomato.

"And that's what happened," said the man. "At first I thought it was the spaghetti eating my wife, which was bad enough, but it was actually the sauce."

"That's very disturbing," Mason agreed.

"I suppose in the future I could just top the noodles with butter, or alfredo sauce, but it just won't be the same."

Mason left the house with the sewing machine the man had sold him for a great price because his wife didn't need it anymore. He was no closer to an answer about how these tomatoes could be stopped.

"Hey!" a woman shouted at him. She hurried

across the street. "I'm Lois Fairchild, from the Times. What's this deal about tomatoes?"

"No comment," said Mason.

"Look, buddy, don't try and stonewall me. How serious is this situation?"

"No comment."

"The American public has a right to know."

Mason sighed with frustration. "If there was a problem, I'd comment on it. My lack of a comment means that everything is fine. Read between the lines, lady."

"That's not how 'no comment' works," said Lois.

"Of course it is. If people were being killed by tomatoes, I'd have plenty of comments. You couldn't get me to stop talking about it. But the situation is so thoroughly under control that not a single comment comes to mind when you ask about it."

"So," said Lois, "there *is* a situation to get under control!"

"No!" said Mason. "Is the number of people who've been killed by tomatoes greater than zero? Yes. But that doesn't mean the tomato apocalypse is nigh. Instead of writing about the number of people who've been killed by tomatoes, why don't you write about the number of people who haven't been killed by tomatoes? The earth's current population is 4.281 billion. Let's round it down to four billion. By our estimate, fewer than a thousand people have lost their lives to tomatoes. That leaves a *lot* of people unkilled."

"Almost a thousand people have died?" asked Lois.

"That's not what I said. Look, on any given day, somebody is going to take too big of a bite out of a tomato and choke to death. Is that newsworthy?"

"No."

"And what if somebody slipped on a tomato? Is that newsworthy?"

"No."

"And what if a tomato ate somebody. Is that newsworthy?"

"Yes."

"Argh!" Mason loathed these journalists and their mind games. "Ma'am, I appreciate you taking the time to accost me in the street, but I have a lot of work to do. Goodbye."

Mason stormed off.

"You can't ignore the press!" Lois shouted after him.

Mason ignored her.

"You can't ignore the press!" Lois repeated, chucking a pinecone at the back of his head.

Mason pretended to ignore her as he continued storming off.

He got into his car, where his special agents waited. Gretta Attenbaum, swimming expert, sat in the back. Next to her was Greg Colburn, underwater expert, his flippers dangling out of the open window. And sitting up front was Abraham Lincoln.

As Mason drove off, he suddenly remembered that Abraham Lincoln had been assassinated 113 years ago. Was this his ghost, trapped on earth until he was able to bring his murderer to justice?

No, wait. As Mason took a closer look, he saw that it was Sam Smith, disguise expert. He was so good at his job that not even the melanin spoiled the illusion.

Mason turned on the radio. "That was The Tie-Wearing Accountants with their smash hit 'Baby, I'll Do Your Taxes and Rock Your World.' And now the song that's sweeping the nation, it's Ronny Desmond with 'Puberty Love.'"

Puberty.
Puberty love.
Puberty.
Puberty love.
Puberty.
Puberty love.

Mason turned off the radio. He hated that song. It was like pouring bleach into his eyes except with his ears.

He dropped Gretta and Greg off to complete their special assignments. Then, to his shock and amazement, he realized that sitting next to him in the passenger seat of his automobile was none other than Adolph Hitler.

Mason wasn't sure what to do. He didn't speak German, and wouldn't have wanted to have a polite conversation with the mad dictator anyway. Mason nervously drummed his fingers on the steering wheel as he tried to figure out what to do. "So, uh, how does it feel to know that if we invent time travel, somebody will try to go back and kill you as a baby?" he asked.

"*Sauerkraut*," said Hitler.

Mason narrowed his eyes. That was a German word, yes, but also one that everybody in America would know, and it definitely didn't answer his question.

He realized that it wasn't Adolph Hitler at all. It was Sam Smith, disguise expert.

"Good one," Mason said.

"*Danke Schön.*"

"Why Hitler? Why not disguise yourself as somebody everybody loves, like Captain Kangaroo?"

"A black Captain Kangaroo? That's crazy talk."

They arrived at the meeting spot: a dirt road out in the middle of nowhere, the kind of place where you

JEFF STRAND

could easily film without permits. There was no sign of Lieutenant Finletter.

"Where could he be?" asked Mason.

~~Hitler~~ Sam Smith shrugged.

"I don't see a car coming in either direction," said Mason. "I guess he pulled a no-show. What are we supposed to do now?"

There was a loud thump as something landed on top of the car.

Mason's first thought was that it was a tomato, and he did not react with great dignity. Then something spilled over the side of the car. A parachute?

Mason's second thought was that the tomatoes were using parachutes now, and he screamed.

Then a man fell off the car, dressed like a paratrooper.

Mason and Sam got out of the car. "So you're Finletter, huh? I'm Mason Dixon."

"Like the demarcation line separating Pennsylvania, Maryland, Delaware, and West Virginia?"

"Yes."

"Pleased to meet you," said Finletter. Then his eyes widened. "Oh my God, it's Adolph Hitler!"

"No," said Mason. "It's—"

Finletter drew his sword. "I always knew this day would come. People laughed at me for all the years I spent training to kill Hitler. 'He's already dead!' they said. 'And even if he wasn't, he'd be eighty-nine years old by now! How much training do you really need to battle an eight-nine-year-old man?' Well, I'll show them!"

"That's not Hitler," said Mason.

"Of course it is! Look at that mustache!" Finletter took a swing with his sword. "That was a practice swing, because I'm still twenty feet away. But there's a special place in Hell for you, Hitler. And I don't

60

mean special in a good way. I mean that you'll have twice as many demons jabbing at you with pitchforks!"

"Remove your disguise before this gets out of hand!" Mason told Sam.

Sam tugged at his mustache. "It won't come off!"

"Of course it won't!" said Finletter. "The real Hitler wouldn't be able to just rip off his mustache!"

Finletter raised his sword and charged at Sam. Mason grabbed one of the cords of his parachute, yanking him off-balance. Finletter tried to get back up, but got caught in his parachute, delivering a few minutes of wacky slapstick antics.

"He's not Hitler," said Mason. "He's a master of disguise."

Finletter crawled out from under his parachute. "Now that I'm getting a closer look, you're right. Hitler's ears were bigger. And this guy doesn't smell like wiener schnitzel."

"I have an idea," Mason told Sam. "Why don't you disguise yourself as a tomato? Infiltrate their camp. Learn their secrets."

"I'm on it," said Sam, hurrying off.

"Shouldn't you have offered him a ride back into town?" asked Finletter. "It's eighteen miles."

"He'll be okay. He can disguise himself as a Jeep."

"Is he really that good?"

Mason nodded. "He's the best."

CHAPTER 10

New York City. (The one in New York state.)

Jim Richardson stepped into the office of Mind Maker and walked up to the receptionist's desk. "Mr. Richardson to see Mr. Swann."

"Yes, sir," said the receptionist. "He's expecting you. I'll let him know you're here. Please have a seat."

Jim sat down on the couch.

The receptionist pressed the button on the intercom. "Mr. Swann? Mr. Richardson is here to see you." She looked over at Jim. "He'll be right with you."

"Thank you," said Jim.

He sat there for a moment.

"Our exchange seemed a bit light on the gags," he said.

"I noticed that, too," said the receptionist. "But I think we just needed to give the reader a breather. You can't have all peaks and no valleys."

"That's true, that's true," said Jim. "Maybe we should do an entire chapter without jokes."

"Some reviews would say we already have."

"Well, they can bite me."

A familiar voice called out to him. "Jimbo, bud-dy!" said Swann, walking out of his office. He wore a shirt with a floral pattern and tight white pants that would never go out of style. "How ya doing?"

"Fine," said Jim, who had once had a man killed for calling him Jimbo, though he didn't like to think about that indiscretion from his youth.

"Super, super," said Swann. "Hey, the president tells me you have a situation, Jimbo."

"A minor pickle, yes."

"More like a major *tomato*, am I right? Of course I'm right!" Swann let out a maniacal laugh. "You boys have come to the right place. Come into my office, have a seat on the ol' swivel-chair, and let me give you a peek at Mind Maker in action."

Jim went into Swann's office and sat down. The swivel-chair did seem like it could be fun, but as the press secretary he had to remain mature and keep the chair pointed in one direction. Swann sat behind his desk.

"First, we have to convince the little housewife out there that the tomato that ate the family pet is not dangerous," said Swann. "No problem."

"Are you sure?" asked Jim. "That sounds like it would be a problem. People do get attached to their family pets."

"With Mind Maker on the job, it's not a problem at all," Swann assured him. "It'll be even easier than convincing them that 'little housewife' isn't demean-ing. Second, we have to convince local authorities that the thousands missing from rural communities were merely stranded during their bicentennial pilgrimage to Philadelphia. No problem."

"Is that literally what we're going to try to do? Or is that a hypothetical example?"

"Third…"

"No, no, don't move on to the third one yet. How much of our overall strategy will be focused on the 'stranded during their bicentennial pilgrimage to Philadelphia' thing? I'm not quite certain that I understand the logistics."

"*Third*," said Swann, ignoring him, "the president wants us to do this in such a way that it can be covered up and no one will know it ever happened. No problem."

"I'm still not ready to move on from the second thing," said Jim. "Were you just using the Philadelphia pilgrimage as an example of one of the many strategies we'll employ to explain the missing people? Or were we explaining every single missing person as having gone on a pilgrimage?"

"But he wants us to do this," said Swann, ignoring him again, "and convince 200 million Americans that this disaster is actually a blessing. Now *that's* a challenge."

"I understand what you're saying, Mr. Swann," Jim lied. "Sometimes the president expects the impossible."

Swann slapped him across the face. "I never said it was impossible! I said it was a challenge! Man was put on this earth to meet challenges, my boy!"

"You really think you can do it?"

"Can I do it? Can I do it?" Swann let out another maniacal laugh, much more frightening than the first. "*Some sell. Some buy. And only we know why.*"

"Wait, hold on," said Jim. "Are you doing a musical number?"

"You bet your sweet patootie I am! And now I have to start over. *Some sell. Some buy. And only we know why. The wrapping's more important than the prize!*"

"I'm honestly not comfortable with a musical number right now. I'm not dressed for it."

"Important decisions are made each day. Much too important for the plain folk to make."

Jim wondered where the music was coming from. It was undeniably catchy, but he hadn't seen a record player anywhere.

"They're always in a bind. Depending on us to make up their mind. Swivel your chair, Jim."

"I'd rather—"

"Swivel it, damn you, or I'll stab you in the face!"

Jim spun his chair in a circle.

"Red box. Blue box. A red box and a blue box. Bright colors and a coupon on the side. Tap your feet when I'm singing to you, goddammit, or I'll tear your throat out with my teeth!"

Jim tapped his feet in time to the music.

"Hard sell or soft sell, it's all the time. Millions of dollars are spent every day. Where do they all go? Mind Maker is here to run the show!"

"Are you sure it's okay to be using these lyrics in a book?" Jim asked. "I know the rights to these things can be kind of tricky. I'd hate to see us get hit with a copyright infringement suit."

"We sell cars and toys for girls and boys. And chairs and beds and shrunken heads. Sugar beets and baseball cleats. And ice to Eskimos."

Swann let out a deranged cackle. His pupils were dilated. His whole body twitched.

"Leeks and mink and boats that sink. No matter what, we'll get it sold."

"Mr. Swann, I think you should take a break from the song," said Jim. "You seem to be getting overstimulated. Maybe just sit down for a few minutes. Have a glass of water. Your face is looking dangerously red."

"We'll use catchy jingles, snappy tunes, and pretty

girls with big balloons. A little lie, a stretch of truth, can turn the public's head. There's TV types and ad execs, and everyone's the best..."

Jim reached across the desk and pressed the intercom button. "Receptionist! I need you to call 911 immediately. I think Mr. Swann is about to have a stroke."

"No!" Mr. Swann grabbed Jim's hand and yanked it away. "You touch that again and I'll break every one of your fingers, and then I'll break the fingers of everyone you've ever cared about! I'm getting to the big finish. It's glorious. I spent hours writing it."

"You weren't ad-libbing this?"

"Of course I wasn't ad-libbing this! People don't just break into a song that they're making up on the spot. There was a lot of prep work involved here. Don't be a simpleton, Jimbo."

"All right. Continue."

"Dance along with me."

"I'd rather not."

"Dance or I'll rip out your ribcage and dump you into an alligator pit."

"I'll dance a little."

"*And yet...they all look up...to a single man...and that one single man is...*"

Jim thought he knew, but didn't want to say anything in case he was wrong.

"*...me!*"

Jim had it completely wrong. He'd thought it was Alice Cooper.

"*They sell, they buy, and only I know why. The human mind is putty in my hands.*"

"The song isn't over?"

"*Important decisions are made each day. Much too important for the plain folk to make.*"

"Wait, did you start over? You're not singing it

again, are you? Please tell me we're not in an infinite time-loop."

"*They're always in a bind. Depend on me to help make up their mind. Decision-wise, policy-wise, demographically speaking...*"

"Credit where it's due. Good job working the word 'demographically' into song lyrics."

"*Mind Maker!*"

The music stopped. Swann dropped to the floor, gasping for breath. "Defibrillators..." he wheezed.

A few shocks later, Swann was back to normal. "Well, let's go meet that challenge, young man. I've already put my staff to work, so if you'd be good enough to stop by in the morning, we can take a look-see at some of the preliminary sketches."

"Then I can tell the president you've accepted the assignment?" asked Jim. As soon as he asked the question, he realized how dumb it was. Swann hadn't done a full musical number just to tell him no.

"You bet your wind-up monkey I've accepted it!" said Swann. "Do you want to see some of my most recent work? I have a public service announcement about how blind police officers can direct traffic as well as anyone, if you just give them a chance."

"That won't be necessary."

"And one about how Nunzio's Potato Chips are the smart choice for consumers who want to stay on good terms with the mob."

"I really should get back to D.C."

"And one proving that sexy women just can't get enough of that Sawyer's auto insurance."

"That one I'll watch."

CHAPTER 11

A sidewalk outside of a hotel. (Somewhere in the USA. They aren't paying me enough to keep up with all of this geography.)

"Sir," said Finletter to Mason, as he tried to hammer tent spikes into the concrete. "I really don't think this is a good place to camp."

"We're not sleeping on the sidewalk," said Mason. It concerned him that Finletter thought they were going to set up a tent out here. That was the behavior of somebody who suffered from legitimate mental health problems. The man needed to be on medication, or at least see a therapist. What kind of a man would try to drive tent spikes into a concrete sidewalk? And why was he still in his paratrooper outfit with the parachute still attached? Was Finletter a danger to himself and others?

"We're not?"

"We're staying in that hotel over there."

"No campfire, sir?"

"No campfire." Had Finletter really believed that they were going to set up a campfire out here on the sidewalk? Mason was deeply worried about his mental and emotional state. He wondered what kind of tragic backstory this poor man had to make him this way. The whole thing made Mason very sad.

"Then what am I supposed to do with these marshmallows?" Finletter asked, holding up the bag.

Mason wanted to cry, but fought back the tears. He promised himself that when this was all over, he'd get Lieutenant Finletter the help he so desperately needed.

———

Lois Fairchild sat in the hotel lobby, pretending to read a newspaper article about people who got sexual excitement out of dressing up like animals, and the people who got sexual excitement out of hunting them for sport. She perked up as Mason Dixon walked into the hotel, followed by a man carrying a parachute. She felt bad for the poor man, who'd clearly had a life full of challenges, and wanted to give him some spare change. But she was trying to remain undercover.

"Here's the key to the room," Mason said to the mentally ill man. "I'm going to check for messages."

Lois knew that the parachute-carrying man's attempt to board the elevator without getting tangled up in his parachute would be visually interesting, but she had to focus on the task at hand. She watched as Mason walked over to the front desk.

"Pardon me," he said to the hotel clerk. "Do you have any messages for Mason Dixon in room…" Lois couldn't hear the room number.

"Which room was that again, sir?"

"Room [*inaudible*]."

"Room [*unintelligible*]?"

"Yes, ma'am."

"Let me check." The hotel clerk checked for messages. "I'm sorry. Nothing for room 807."

"That's not the room number I said. I said [*unhearable*]."

"My mistake." The clerk checked again. "I'm sorry. No messages for that particular room."

"Are you sure? I was expecting a message left under my room number."

Lois hoped that Mason wouldn't notice that she was only a few inches away from him.

"I've checked your room number, and also the room numbers with the same digits in different combinations, just in case the message got filed incorrectly. There's nothing. Maybe you're less popular than you believed?"

"Thanks for your help," said Mason, walking away from the front desk.

"May I help you?" the clerk asked Lois.

"Could you tell me what room Mason Dixon is staying in?"

"The privacy of our guests is very important to us. How do I know you're not a serial killer or a reporter?"

"I'm his sister."

"You don't look anything like him."

"I mean, I'm his wife."

"You're too attractive to be his wife."

"I'm his mistress."

"Same problem."

"I'm his employee."

"That one works, but since it's your fourth try, I have to assume that you're making all of this up."

"Fine. My name is Lois Fairchild. I'm a reporter from the Daily Herald. I'm covering a story of worldwide importance, exposing what the government is trying to keep hidden from the public, and Mr. Dixon is being uncooperative. I need his room number so I can fool the hotel clerk into giving me his key. Then I can sneak into his room in the middle of the night and see if he has any incriminating papers lying around."

The clerk nodded. "It's a solid plan. What story are you covering?"

"I'm not at liberty to say."

"You're being secretive about your efforts to expose government secrets. You have become that which you believed you were fighting."

"I'm writing about the killer tomatoes."

"Like the ones that ate my nephew?"

"Yes! A lot of nephews have died, and even more nephews will die if the American people are kept in the dark about this menace."

The clerk placed a key on the front desk. "It would be unprofessional of me to tell you which room Mr. Dixon is staying in. But I'll give you the key to his room, and with some trial and error, you'll eventually find what you're looking for. I just hope you aren't irreversibly corrupted in the process."

"Thank you," said Lois, taking the key. "I'm sorry about your nephew."

"It's okay. He was studying to become a lawyer. But not one of those universally beloved lawyers—an unpopular one."

"Still, I'm sorry." Lois headed toward the elevator. She had a lot of doors to check.

———

When Mason stepped out of the bathroom, freshly showered and plucked, Finletter was seated on the couch, still wrapped in his parachute, watching television.

"Pray-Tel presents, Voices From Beyond The Grave," said the commercial announcer. *"Twenty-one songs from artists who are dead, dead, dead. In the ground! Breathing no more! Jimi Hendrix! Dead! Janis Joplin! Dead! And nineteen more, performing the hit songs they recorded before their demise! Operators are standing by! Enjoy this while you can, because soon technology is going to make the art of the mix tape obsolete, and you'll just listen to random songs with no ebb or flow! I don't want to live in that world, so I plan to be dead, dead, dead, just like Buddy Holly and Jim Croce! Order now!"*

"Turn that off, and let's get some sleep," said Mason.

Finletter turned off the television. "Marshmallow?" he offered.

It was a cruel reminder of the time, not long ago, when Finletter had believed that they were going to sleep in a tent on the sidewalk, having a campfire and roasting marshmallows. The poor man was so very damaged. Could he even be fixed, or was it too late? The sights he must have seen. The horrors he must have experienced. Trauma was no laughing matter, and Finletter had clearly endured far more than his share.

"Why are you crying?" Finletter asked.

"I'm not," said Mason, wiping his eyes. He knew this man would never want to be pitied.

———

Lois had tried to unlock every door in the hotel except 401. In retrospect, she should have checked the doors sequentially instead of randomly, but she was still a new journalist and a lot of the tricks of the trade came from experience.

Not everybody who stayed in a hotel kept their

door locked. There had been a great many awkward moments. If she never had to hear, "Hey, join right in!" again, it would be too soon.

She slid the key into the lock. It fit. She twisted the doorknob. It turned.

Moving very slowly so as not to alert Mason and the parachute man that she was sneaking uninvited into their room to invade their privacy, Lois pushed the door open.

The parachute man was on the couch, wide awake.

Of course he was wide awake. The poor thing probably saw nightmarish images every time he closed his eyes. Sleep was a rare commodity.

It occurred to Lois that she probably should have come up with a contingency plan in case she got caught. Something like trying to convince the parachute man that she was an anxiety-induced hallucination. Instead, she stepped back, stammering.

"Oh, I'm terribly sorry," she said. "I—I mean, I thought this was your...I mean our...I mean your...I mean my...I'm surprised as you are that my room key opened up your room. We'll want to talk to the hotel about that. They're probably saving money by using the same keys for all the rooms. Sorry. I'm going now."

She quickly left, closing the door behind her.

That had been close. *Too* close. There was no saying what an emotionally damaged paratrooper might have done upon seeing a stranger entering his room. But she wasn't giving up.

———

"Who was that?" asked Mason, stepping out of the bedroom.

"I believe it was a prostitute, sir."

"You're done already?"

"I didn't make use of her services."

"Why would a prostitute show up at our room?"

Finletter shrugged. "Maybe the front desk sent her up as a courtesy."

"This hotel was too affordable for that. Are you sure that's what she was?"

"Well, she could have been a strumpet, harlot, or trollop."

"Go back to sleep, Finletter."

———

A phone call woke Mason up from a pleasant dream about a complimentary escort showing up at his hotel room. "Hmm?" he answered. "What? Where? I'll be right there!" He hung up and quickly got out of bed.

As the author of this novelization, I apologize for not being able to share what was said on the other end of the phone conversation. I have access to a lot of inside information, stuff that would *shock* you, but not everything. I'm hoping that this lack of a transcript won't cause confusion.

Mason hurried out of the bedroom. Finletter had breakfast waiting. Mason wondered, with no small degree of concern, if that meal had been prepared for Mason, or the ghosts of Finletter's departed friends who no doubt haunted him.

"Listen, this is important," said Mason. "You've got to go down and warn Gretta that there's tomato activity in Sector Two. You got that?"

Oh, good. That's what the phone call was about. I was worried that I'd be remiss in providing my expository duties, but now we're all caught up.

"Got it, sir," said Finletter. "Will you be joining me for breakfast?"

"No time!" Mason sprinted out of the hotel room. Finletter realized that Mason had forgotten to take his vitamins. Oh well. More for him.

CHAPTER 12

Manhattan.

Young Billy relaxed against the oak tree, fishing for trout in the pond by his country home. Peaceful music played in the background. His loyal hound dog, Spot, sat next to him.

Spot's ears perked up at a sound in the distance. Something rustled in the bushes.

"What is it, Spot?" asked Billy. "What's in there?"

"Gosh, Billy, I don't know," said Spot. "You stay there. I'll go look."

Billy nodded. Usually when his dog spoke to him it was to tell him that Spot needed another human sacrifice, so this was a welcome change.

Spot hurried off into the bushes.

Billy stood up. Something was babbling in the bushes. His beloved dog was in danger!

———

Soon the only thing left of Billy was his fishing rod, abandoned on the shore of the pond.

Though the young boy died a horrible death, Spot the Dog was perfectly fine. He escaped the killer tomatoes injury-free, and after a few adventures wandering the Manhattan countryside was adopted by a loving family. They treated their new pet well, feeding him only the highest quality dog food, and Spot lived out the rest of his years happy and warm.

A military encampment. Castle Rock, Maine.

"What are those red circles, sir?" asked Private Reptilicis, tapping his index finger on the map.

"Machine gun emplacements," said Captain Triffid. "We've got the whole valley surrounded with them. I don't think we can hold them off for very long, though."

"And that green line. That's their furthest point of advance?"

"That's right."

"What are the blue dots?"

"Those are Mobil stations."

"Good, good. We'll need plenty of gas for this operation. And that chartreuse spiral?"

"It looks pretty. Livens the map up."

"It certainly does. What's that white stripe?"

"It's the edge of the map."

"And the invisible flaming dragon face?"

"Your imagination."

A jeep drove into the encampment. Not by itself, obviously; somebody was driving it.

"That must be Major Mills," said Captain Triffid. "Take over the map analysis."

Triffid hurried over to the jeep. Major Mills was indeed inside the jeep, along with another man Triffid didn't recognize, though if we switch to omniscient point-of-view we can say that it was Mason Dixon.

"I'm glad you could make it, sir," said Triffid, who was relieved that the jeep didn't have doors, sparing him the awkward moment of not being sure if he should open the door for the major or not. "I think we've got something that will interest you. No promises, obviously. I don't want to build it up too much and disappoint you."

Mills and Mason got out of the jeep. Triffid led them to the science section of the encampment, where a man in a white lab coat was doing scientific things to their discovery.

Mason's mouth dropped open at what he saw.

It couldn't be!

But it was! Right there in front of him!

"Sir, we've captured a giant tomato," said Triffid, spoiling the surprise.

This tomato was the size of a pumpkin. Not a prize-winning county fair pumpkin, but a pumpkin of sufficient size that any household would proudly display as a jack-o-lantern on their front porch at Halloween.

But that was okay. They could handle pumpkin-sized tomatoes. This was no worse than if pumpkins became sentient and started eating people. Mason was confident that the military could eradicate this threat.

"It's worse than we thought," said the scientist.

"How can it be worse?" Mills asked. "Normal-sized tomatoes are growing to the size of basketballs! There's no way you can share an observation that makes me more cynical about the survival of the human race!"

The scientist gave him a grim nod. "This, may God help us, is only a cherry tomato."

Everybody in the encampment stress-vomited.

———

A woman screamed as a tomato the size of a Volkswagen Beetle (prior to its heartbreaking redesign) chased her across the parking lot.

Trigger Warning: You may have been under the impression that this was a book about normal-sized tomatoes killing people. And until now, it had been. But those pages are over, and this is now the terrifying tale of *giant* tomatoes killing people. You think you can handle it, but you can't. It's okay. There's no shame in cowardice. If you continue reading, you will wake up screaming every night for the rest of your life, however long that may be. (I know how long, but I'm not authorized to share that information.)

Don't do it. Don't read any further. Choose something lighter, like *Where the Red Fern Grows*. No good can come of this.

———

Milk (2%)
Bread (wheat)
Apples (granny smith if available)
Paper napkins (super absorbent; eye-pleasing pattern)
Cheese (pepperjack)

Wait, are you still reading this? Didn't I dissuade you?

Here's the deal: The book is too frightening for you, and if you flee in terror, I don't have to finish writing it. It's win/win. Go read a different book, or watch a movie, or play outdoors with the cartoon squirrels, or invent a refreshing beverage. Go live your life.

Grapes (seedless)
Grapes (extra seeds)
Mayonnaise (crunchy-style)

You're not going anywhere, are you? All right. Fine. Don't come crying to me later. "Waahhh! My brain doesn't work anymore because I'm so scared!" You were warned.

Just do me a favor and try to read slowly so that I can stay ahead of you. Thanks.

———

Sector Two.

Gretta sat in a forest clearing, enjoying a hearty bowl of steroids with milk. She couldn't help but feel that her skills as a swimming expert were being wasted out here in the middle of the forest, but she was not one to question orders, regardless of who they came from.

A noise.

It sounded like a large rolling object.

But that was ridiculous. There were no large rolling objects in the forest.

It definitely wasn't a tomato. Tomatoes were small.

The large rolling object was getting closer. Gretta stood up. Whatever it was, she would use all of her skills to defeat it, even though all of her skills involved swimming.

The object came into view. It was a *great big giant tomato!!!!!!!* Coming *right at her!!!!!!!!!!!!*

It was the size of a beach ball. A large beach ball, not a small one. The kind a rich kid would have if his parents never had to say, "No, no, my darling son, the small beach ball is cheaper."

Gretta kicked the tomato out of the way. It flew into the air and disappeared amongst the trees. Wait…was she good at kicking? Was this a skill she'd been unaware of all her life? She'd been so focused on her swimming abilities that it had never really occurred to her that her feet were good for other things.

Another giant tomato rolled into the clearing.

Gretta kicked it so hard that it split in half. Tomato gook sprayed everywhere.

"Take that, veggie-face!" she shouted. She wished she'd shouted something cleverer, but apparently her skills were limited to swimming and kicking, not snappy one-liners after destroying a tomato.

Another tomato rolled into the clearing. She sent it flying back into the air from whence it came.

"Take that, veggie-face!" she shouted at it. "Do any more of you veggie-faces want to take that?"

A tomato rolled toward her, followed immediately by another one. This was concerning. She hadn't anticipated that the production budget would allow for two tomatoes at once.

She kicked the first tomato, which smacked into the second tomato. The tomatoes babbled with fury.

A third tomato rolled into the clearing. Gretta clenched her fists. Maybe she could punch, too.

She punched the third tomato. Unfortunately, she couldn't remember what she'd shouted at the others after hurting them, so she decided to remain silent rather than risk shouting something inferior.

The first tomato came at her again. Despite the image on the movie poster/book cover, tomatoes didn't have faces. But she kicked it where she assumed its face would be.

Her foot broke through its skin, sinking deep into the tomato's insides. Slime poured out of it. Gretta couldn't imagine how disgusting and disturbing this must be for the other tomatoes. If her foot broke through a human being, causing its guts to become visible, she'd be sick to her stomach right now.

Gretta tried to pull her foot loose.

[*Editor's Note:* "Foot loose." "Footloose." People like the movie *Footloose*. You should be able to get at least six or seven good *Footloose* gags in here. What about the whole "Six Degrees of Kevin Bacon" thing? Kevin Bacon was in *Footloose*. There's bacon in a BLT sandwich. There's tomato in a BLT sandwich. Brilliant, huh?]

[*Author's Note:* What are you talking about? What's *Footloose*? Who's Kevin Bacon? I've never heard of either of these things in 1978.]

[*Editor's Note:* I've said too much.]

Gretta tried to pull her foot loose, but it was stuck inside the tomato. She yanked as hard as she could. Her foot wouldn't budge.

Another tomato launched itself at her. She punched it in mid-air, and her fist burst through the skin, trapping her entire arm inside of the vegetable.

"Take that, veggie-head!" she shouted. No, wait, that wasn't right.

The tomato was surprisingly heavy, and her arm fell to her side with the tomato still attached.

Another tomato attacked.

She kicked it with her free foot. This time, she didn't break through, but the tomato only rolled a short distance away. It came right back, faster this time, and she kicked it again. It was such a mighty kick that her leg went all the way through the immense beast, popping out on the other side.

It was extremely difficult to walk with a tomato on each leg. Gretta fell over.

A tomato flew at her head.

Gretta screamed.

Everything went dark. Not *completely* dark, but gloomy and blurry, the way it would look if your head was buried inside of a giant tomato. Gretta couldn't breathe. She knew that her only chance was to eat her way out.

She did her best, but her jaws were not up to the task.

RIP Gretta Attenbaum. She deserved more screen time.

The tomatoes eventually pulled themselves away from her and rolled to the hospital garden for medical attention.

———

Lieutenant Finletter stepped into the clearing. He gazed upon Gretta's body. He jabbed at her with his sword, but since there was nothing left except her blue jumpsuit, some bones, and a scrap of flesh or two, he suspected that she had not survived the encounter.

Finletter decided not to bother delivering the warning.

CHAPTER 13

Jim Richardson stepped into the office of Mind Maker and walked up to the receptionist's desk. "Mr. Richardson to see Mr. Swann."

"Yes, sir," said the receptionist. "He's expecting you. I'll let him know you're here. Please have a seat."

Jim sat down on the couch.

The receptionist pressed the button on the intercom. "Mr. Swann? Mr. Richardson is here to see you." She looked over at Jim. "He'll be right with you."

"Thank you," said Jim.

He sat there for a moment.

"Does replaying the exact same joke-free scene count as a joke?" he asked.

"I don't think it does," the receptionist admitted. "We'd need some sort of twist."

"It's too late now. Should we try again?"

"That might be a bit self-indulgent."

"I'd rather be accused of self-indulgence than not caring."

"That's fair. Let's try one more time."

Jim Richardson stepped into the office of Mind Maker, wearing an unbelievably silly hat, and walked up to the receptionist's desk. "Mr. Richardson to see Mr. Swann."

"Yes, sir," said the receptionist. "He's expecting you. I'll let him know you're here. Please have a seat. My goodness, that may be the zaniest head-wear I've seen in my life. Look at all those colors and textures. I never knew they made hats quite that nutty."

"It's quite a sight gag, isn't it?" asked Jim, as he sat down on the couch.

The receptionist pressed the button on the inter-com. "Mr. Swann? Mr. Richardson is here to see you, and just wait until you see his hat!" She looked over at Jim. "He'll be right with you."

"Thank you," said Jim. He removed the hat. It had served its purpose.

"Jimbo!" said Swann, walking into the waiting area. "How's it going?"

"I believe that's my question." He didn't like being rude, but Swann needed to remember who worked for the president, and who worked for the man who worked for the president.

"Right, right! Come into my office, and I'll show you what we've come up with. Mind Maker at its best!"

Jim followed Swann into his office. He sat down, mildly disappointed that the swivel-chair had been replaced by a normal non-swivel chair.

"The first thing we need are slogans," said Swann. "People love slogans! When was the last time you bought a product that didn't have a catchy slogan? Never, right? Products without slogans can go straight to hell. Well, the same thing applies to disas-ters! We just have to make the death and destruction seem fun!"

"I'm listening."

"How about this one? 'Giant tomatoes mean bigger pizzas.' Genius, huh?"

"Is it, though?" asked Jim. "Pizza size isn't really dependent on tomato size."

"Okay, okay."

"It's not like you serve pizza on a great big slice of tomato. Their size is irrelevant. Also, that one poor guy died from drinking tomato juice, so presumably eating a pizza with tomato sauce would be equally fatal."

"You're missing the bigger picture," said Swann. "It's not about accuracy or logic. It's about lying to the public in an appealing manner."

"Ah, I now understand the satirical point you're trying to make. Continue."

Swann pressed play on a cassette player. *"If you're feeling sad and blue, tomatoes end it all for you."*

"Nice," said Jim. "I'm sure there's a downside to a pro-suicide jingle, but I can't think of one right now."

The tape continued. An announcer said, *"Last year, more people were killed by automobile accidents, heart attacks, lung cancer, and natural causes combined, than any one tomato."*

Jim nodded. "I like it. He has an accent-free voice that you can trust."

"And what if, hear me out, our lord and savior Jesus Christ himself assured the nation that there was nothing to fear?"

"Is he available?"

"We'd hire an actor. One with gravitas."

"How blasphemous would it be?"

"Just blasphemous enough."

"That's great," said Jim. "People do like Jesus. What else have you got?"

"We've got a logo, but it's really more of a sight gag."

"No need to show me, then. I think the president will be very pleased with your progress so far."

"And we've only just begun," said Swann. "Wait until you see our 'Your Deceased Family Members Were Merely Figments of Your Imagination' campaign."

"Amazing."

"We're also trying to figure out a way to place the blame entirely on vegans."

"Clever."

"And finally, this poster will be in every bus station and subway car across the nation." Swann held up a poster that showed a giant tomato on one side, and a nuclear power plant oozing glowing green radiation on the other. A tagline said, "It Could Be Much Worse."

"Hmmm," said Jim.

"What's wrong?" asked Swann. "People don't say 'hmmm' unless they're noncommittal about something."

"It sort of looks like you're saying that nuclear power caused the giant killer tomatoes."

Swann looked at the poster. "So it does. I'll have the designer executed."

Jim chuckled.

"I'm not kidding. I'll hire an assassin to kill him and leave a few tomatoes by his dead body to throw the authorities off the track."

"That's not necessary," said Jim. "Incompetence should only be a death sentence if you're a clumsy firefighter."

"Fine. The designer lives. For now."

———

Could nothing stop this tomato onslaught?

Los Angeles, California.

People ran screaming from the killer tomatoes.

———

Boston, Massachusetts.

People ran screaming from the killer tomatoes.

Seattle, Washington.

People ran screaming from the killer tomatoes.

———

Chicago, Illinois.

People ran screaming from the killer tomatoes.

———

Even the mere mention of the word was sufficient to induce panic.

Angus sat in the crowded library, relishing the power he wielded. With one word—one!—he could unleash chaos amongst the patrons. Oh, the sweet, sweet anarchy.

But did he dare?

Yes. He dared.

Angus looked to the left. Then he looked to the right. These book-reading fools didn't suspect a thing.

He took a deep breath.

"Tomato," he said.

The library patrons screamed, leapt to their feet, and fled, scattering books and papers everywhere. It was glorious pandemonium.

Angus smiled as he sat alone in the library.

And then the self-loathing set in.

Why had he done that? Somebody could've gotten hurt. They could've been trampled. They could've even been killed. He'd done it all for a prank—for an *amusement*. He'd put the safety of innocent library-goers in danger just because he thought it would be fun to say "tomato."

He was reprehensible. Human garbage.

Unworthy of love.

Angus placed his head down on the desk and wept for several minutes.

It wasn't too late for him to change. It was *never* too late to change. Now that he recognized he was a monster, he'd achieved the first step in becoming a better person. There were many more steps to go, and it would require a lot of hard work on his part, but he knew deep inside that he could fix himself.

Angus wiped away his tears, stood up, and looked for the self-help section.

As Mason Dixon drove around town, his thoughts were stressing him out.

Everybody's gonna get eaten by tomatoes, his thoughts said. *Even you! Especially you!*

He politely asked his thoughts to knock it off, because they weren't helping anything.

Oh, are we upsetting you? his thoughts asked. *Is our focus on death by tomatoes making you uncomfortable?*

Should we try to take you to your happy place? That magical beach where you can sip margaritas all day long? Okay, Mason, here's a margarita for you. Take a nice big sip. Oh no! It was a bloody Mary! Your happy place is filled with sadness and horror!

Mason turned on the radio to distract himself.

Argh! Foiled again! You may have won this round, Mason, but we'll be back!

"Hey, hey, hey," said the DJ, though emphatically not in a Fat Albert voice, "you're listening to the rocking sounds of 108.1 FM! That was 'Your Kiss Missed' by Banjo Dan & The Yaks. Before that was 'Burnt Spleen Blues' by Men Who Drink Coffee. And before that was 'Them Grits Ain't Cooked Right' by We Aren't Particularly Good at Making Music But At Least We're Honest About It Unlike Some Other Bands We Could Name. And before that was 'Hey, Satan, You Suck' by God's Rockers. Before that we played 'Grampa Broke the Outhouse' by The Missing Teeth. Right before that was 'Your Kiss Missed (Acoustic Version)' by Banjo Dan & The Yaks. And coming up next, it's the hit song that fans are burning down radio stations for playing insufficiently, 'Puberty Love' by Ronny Desmond."

Suddenly, Mason realized that he needed his thoughts again and shut off the radio. A gigantic tomato was right in front of his car, blocking his path!

Mason put the car into reverse, but a gigantic tomato was behind him, too!

He rolled down the window. "Shoo!" he shouted.

The tomatoes did not shoo.

He was going to have to floor the gas pedal and splatter one of these tomatoes.

Mason needed mood music if he was going to perform an action sequence. He turned the radio back on.

Puberty.
Puberty love.
Puberty.
Puberty love.
Puberty.
Puberty love.

The tomato in front of the car rolled away.

Mason turned around. The tomato behind him was also gone.

He stroked his chin to show that he was deep in thought. What had just happened was very peculiar, but what did it mean? What information could be gleaned from this experience?

Mason shrugged. Probably nothing.

CHAPTER 14

The Pentagon. (Washington, D.C. or vicinity.)

"So that's what happened," said Mason, recapping the end of the previous chapter. "I got out of there as fast as I could."

"You made no unusual motions of any kind?" asked Dr. Nokitofa, still badly dubbed.

"Not as far as I know."

"Odd."

Dr. Morrison leaned forward. "Were there any loud noises or other extraneous activity that might have affected the tomatoes' behavior, such as an airplane, another car in the vicinity, or a helpless screaming child?"

"I'm almost sure there wasn't."

"Almost only counts in horseshoes, hand grenades, and brain surgery."

"I'm sure there wasn't."

"What about music?" asked Dr. Morrison. "Was any music playing?"

"I don't recall," said Mason.

"Are you the type of man who drives with the radio on, or with the radio off?"

"I'm inconsistent. The radio *might* have been on."

"And if the radio was on, do you know what particular song might have been playing?"

"I'm not sure," Mason admitted. "It's not the kind of detail that would stick out in my memory."

"It doesn't matter," said Dr. Morrison. "I'm sure it's unimportant."

"Now that I think about it, I'm almost certain that the radio was off. Music was completely irrelevant to my survival."

"That's fine. As scientists, we have to come up with long-shot theories that we know probably won't pan out."

Jim Richardson stood up. "If you'll excuse me, gentlemen, I really have to be getting back to Washington."

"We're in Washington," said Major Mills.

"No, we're in San Diego."

"That's not what the chapter heading says."

"Well, the chapter heading is wrong. When my flight landed, the pilot clearly welcomed me to San Diego."

"Does that mean the heading was also wrong in Chapter Three?"

"I suppose so."

"Can they go back and fix it?"

Jim chuckled. "This book has no budget for rewrites. We can't even fix typoe's."

"Are you sure you can't stay for a few more minutes?" asked Major Mills. "Somebody made pigs-in-a-blanket! And that somebody is me!"

"Sorry."

"That's okay. I mean, I did grind up the beef and pork myself, and I slaughtered the cow and pig with my own hand just to make it extra special, and I wrote everybody's name in the dough before I put it in the oven. You can't read the names anymore because the dough expanded, but the imprint is there, like homeopathic medicine."

"I really do have to get going."

"I burnt myself on the tray," said Major Mills, holding up his blister-covered hand.

Jim cringed. "You really need to be more careful. Those things need lanced."

"My grandmother always told me that oven mitts are a barrier between yourself and the food you're cooking with love."

"Fine," said Jim. "I'll have one of your pigs-in-a-blanket."

"Just one?"

———

Lois Fairchild inserted a dime into the pay phone, happy to live in a time when the phrase "It's your dime" still made sense to America's youth, along with the term "pay phone." She spun the rotary dial, marveling at its convenience.

"Yeah?" answered Conrad, her editor-in-chief, sounding surly.

"Trouble, sir."

"I don't like hearing the word 'trouble' unless it's somebody else's trouble that makes for a good story."

"I haven't seen Mason Dixon all day. I've been following his assistant, but that's getting me nowhere and making me sad."

Conrad sighed. "Look, I thought I made it perfectly clear. I don't think you've made use of your *potential*, if you know what I mean, and what I mean is your boobies. Sorry. That was unprofessional. I meant boobs."

"I resent that, sir."

"Why? I was complimentary about them! Could they be larger and firmer? Sure. But they'll still get the job done."

"I'm not doing it," said Lois.

"All I'm asking you to do is make the guy think you're willing to have sex with him, and then have sex with him, and then use that to get information from him for your story."

"No," said Lois.

"Then what else are you going to use? Your skills as an investigative journalist?" Conrad was silent for a moment. "Wait a minute. We might be on to something. You have a journalism degree, right?"

"Yes, sir."

"So maybe instead of trying to seduce Dixon's assistant, you could talk to him in a manner that *isn't* trying to imply that he's going to get lucky, and acquire the information through the skills they taught you in college, plus the skills you've learned on the job thus far. That's actually a much better idea. The original plan kind of made me look like a chauvinistic pig. Did it make you feel uncomfortable?"

"Yes, sir."

"That's not right. I'm a product of my time, but maybe I should learn to be better than 1978. If you were here in my office right now, I could slap you on the rear end and expect you to giggle and say 'Oh, you!' Yet I'm starting to recognize that I don't slap female employees on the rear because I'm a filthy pervert. I do it because it's a power move. It's not that I enjoy it, but that I can get away with it. I'm not going to do it anymore."

"I'm very glad to hear it, sir," said Lois.

"And maybe I'll tell fewer racist jokes. No Chinese man ever tampered with my Coke."

"Another admirable step."

"Will this change in attitude last beyond this phone call? Probably not. But for now I'm a new man. So forget that closed-minded sexist nonsense about not using your potential. Your breasts are irrelevant. Get that story!"

———

Meanwhile, at a pay phone right next to the one Lois was using, Finletter called Mason. He got the first six numbers correct on the rotary dial but messed up the seventh, forcing him to start over. He didn't mind—he found the sound of the rotary dial quite soothing, and was happy that he was dialing numbers like 7, 8, and 9 more than 1, 2, and 3, because the dial had further to go.

Finally the call went through. "Trouble, sir," he told Mason.

"What kind of trouble? 'Tomatoes have taken over the city' trouble or 'locked yourself out of the hotel room' trouble?"

"Halfway between those two. Well, on the scale you gave me I guess it's closer to locking myself out of the room, but it's a lot worse than that. There's a pretty wide gap between the two kinds of trouble you mentioned, sir."

"Just tell me why you called," said Mason.

"I'm being followed by the woman who entered our room last night. I think she's a spy."

"What kind of spy?"

"Unknown as of yet. Permission to capture and torture her, sir?"

"No. Don't torture anybody."

"Are you sure? Fingernails grow back."

"Permission denied."

"What if it was an elaborate trap, forcing her to choose between two unthinkable options?"

"You sound very stressed," said Mason. "Perhaps you should take a nap."

"A nap, sir?"

"Yes. I'll be back soon. You take yourself a nice little nap, and we'll talk when I get there."

"I don't take naps, sir."

"Because of the horrible things you see when you close your eyes?"

"Excuse me?"

"Just take a nap."

"But I can't do that, sir," said Finletter. "If I did, I'd be napping instead of contributing."

"You'd be conserving your energy for the most opportune time to use it. You're seeing spies. That's not normal behavior. I'm worried that if you don't get some rest, you could snap, and who knows what kind of a body count would result? Severed heads everywhere."

"But naps are for preschoolers."

"No, they're also for old people. And for people like you whose sanity is *riiiiight* on the precipice. One minute you're seeing spies, the next minute you're seeing disembodied ghost faces shimmering in mid-air."

Finletter looked crestfallen. "All right."

"Good," said Mason. "I'll be back soon."

"Operator," said Finletter, "I was very disappointed in that conversation. I'd like my dime back."

"Go take your nap, baby," said the operator.

———

Lois put on her sunglasses as Finletter hung up the phone. The paratrooper shuffled toward the elevator, moving slowly, head hung, shoulders slumped, letting out a deep sigh every few seconds. As a top-notch journalist, Lois could tell that he was bummed out.

"Hey," she said. "I'm sorry about accidentally coming into your room last night. I was super drunk."

"It's okay," said Finletter.

"I'd seen too many advertisements for beer yesterday and couldn't help myself."

Finletter nodded as if the weight of the world was on top of his head, making it difficult to nod. "I understand. May I ask you a question?"

"Yes, I have been on a wild boar hunt, but we didn't catch one."

"That's not what I was going to ask. Are you a spy?"

"No."

"Oh." Finletter frowned. "I'm not sure if a real spy would confirm or deny it."

"Legally, a spy would have to confirm it if they were asked directly."

"Thanks. I'm going to take a nap now. Maybe I'll dream of bunnies."

Finletter pressed the elevator call button, moving as if the weight of the world was on his arm. The doors opened, and he shuffled inside, not bothering to drag his parachute into the elevator with him. Lois pulled it in for him, sparing Finletter the experience of having the doors close with the parachute on the other side, causing him to be pulled to the doors as the elevator rose and eventually snapped in half.

On the fourth floor, Finletter went to his room,

stared at the door for a full minute, and then sadly went inside, leaving the door open behind him.

Lois looked at the open door. An opportunity!

She listened carefully for the sound of Finletter lying down on the couch. She heard the couch cushions creak. Now she just needed to wait for the sound of snoring, or him mumbling disturbing things in his sleep.

There! She'd heard a snore!

Lois crept into the room.

Finletter's left eye opened, followed by his right.

"I knew it!" he shouted, jumping to his feet. "You're a spy!"

Unfortunately for Lois, Finletter slept with his sword, spooning it. He charged at her, missing skewering her by inches. The sword stabbed deep into the wall. Somebody on the other side cried out, but it was probably unrelated.

"Spy!" Finletter shouted, yanking the sword out of the wall. The tip was red, so apparently the adjoining room was painted a different color than this one.

Lois wanted to explain that she wasn't a spy, but that would have used up valuable sword-avoiding time. She grabbed a lamp and threw it at him. Finletter swung his sword, cutting the lamp neatly in half in mid-air.

Lois kicked over the table upon which a tray of breakfast items rested, hoping that Finletter would trip on some of the blueberries as they spilled out of the leftover bowl of oatmeal. Instead, they squished harmlessly under his feet.

Finletter swung the sword at her. One inch closer, and it would've come ten inches from her face.

Lois tried to pick up the couch to use as a weapon, but it seemed to be glued to the floor.

Finletter took several more swings at her. The first

swing destroyed the television, the second destroyed a coffee maker, the third destroyed an iron, the fourth destroyed a hamster, the fifth destroyed a Rembrandt (or perhaps a replica—Lois didn't have an opportunity to verify) and the sixth tore open a pillow, sending feathers flying everywhere.

Lois took off one of her shoes and flung it at him. It struck Finletter in the face.

"It's like you kicked me without using your foot!" said Finletter.

"I'm not a spy," Lois insisted.

"Only a spy, or somebody who legitimately wasn't a spy, would say that!" Finletter charged again. This time he forgot to swing his sword, so he slammed into the wall, knocking a dozen pieces of artwork to the floor.

Lois, realizing that she probably wasn't going to get any good information for her story, fled the room.

Finletter continued to fight for another ten minutes before he realized that his enemy was gone. Then he slipped on some of the remnants of destruction and knocked himself unconscious.

———

When Finletter woke up, Mason was seated on a broken chair.

"Have a good nap?" Mason asked.

"Not really, sir."

"Looks like you trashed the place a bit."

"I was trying to kill a spy, sir."

"I see. And did this spy escape through the hole you made in the floor?"

"I'm not sure. I lost track amidst the slapstick."

Mason nodded. "Did you give Gretta her warning?"

"Yes."

"Was she alive when you did it?"

"No."

"Very upsetting. I would've expected her swimming skills to serve her better."

CHAPTER 15

Sam Smith, disguise expert, looked almost exactly like a giant tomato. If tomatoes could mutate to this size, who was to say that they couldn't also sprout arms, legs, and a human head? He'd been nervous when he arrived at their camp, but they'd welcomed him as a fellow tomato. Now he sat around the campfire as they feasted upon their latest victims.

Though Smith had not yet learned their language, he was able to read the subtitles.

Who's ready for an arm? asked the tomato seated next to him.

Ooh! I am! said the tomato on the other side of him.

Pass it on, said the first tomato, handing a severed arm to Smith. He grimaced, but he knew that if he went "Eeewwww!" it would blow his cover. He handed the arm to the other tomato, trying not to look at the gross part.

The tomato hungrily munched away. Smith thought that the sound of it devouring a human arm was the worst part of the experience, but then he peeked and saw that it was, in fact, not.

Could somebody pass a leg?

A tomato gave Smith a leg, freshly roasted in the campfire. Smith couldn't lie and say that it didn't smell good, but he obviously wasn't tempted to sample it. He passed it along.

My favorite part is the intestines, said the tomato across from him. *They're like spaghetti. So many humans ate us on top of spaghetti, and now we eat their intestines like spaghetti. It's poetic justice. Watch me slurp up the entire thing, end to end, without taking a breath.*

Smith tried not to cringe. It was the most disgusting thing he'd seen since infiltrating that cannibal camp a few years ago.

Aren't you hungry? a tomato asked him.

Smith shook his head.

Why don't you speak?

Smith tried to mimic the weird babbling noises that the tomatoes made. If he was lucky, they'd be able to read his subtitles. *Not hungry.*

Not hungry? What kind of tomato is not hungry?

Had a big lunch. Full of orphans and nuns.

Oh, go on. Have a pancreas.

Later, maybe.

If you don't eat the pancreas, we will have no choice but to be suspicious. We might think that you're not really a tomato, but rather a human being in an incredibly convincing disguise.

Smith gulped.

Should he have done that? Did tomatoes gulp?

All right, he said. *I'll have some pancreas.*

———

Greg Colburn, underwater expert, swam around in a fountain. He'd pretty much been forgotten about, and that's just how he liked it.

————

Mason and Finletter walked along the sidewalk, toward Mason's inconveniently parked vehicle.

A gunshot rang out.

"Did you hear that?" asked Mason.

"Sounded like a gunshot," said Finletter.

"Do you think it was aimed at one of us?"

"No. I assume they were aiming for that bleeding guy just up ahead."

They continued walking.

Another gunshot. A man in front of them cried out, clutched his chest, and fell to the ground.

"I wonder what he did to make somebody shoot him?" said Mason.

"It must've been pretty bad. People don't shoot each other for no reason."

Mason nodded politely to a man who was walking in the other direction. A gunshot struck the man down.

"Wow," said Mason. "That's three. It's crazy to think that we were walking near three people who deserved to die."

"It's a miracle that we weren't hit by accident," said Finletter.

"I know, right?"

————

Military base. (Not the same one where the scientist shared the upsetting news that it was merely a cherry tomato.)

Finletter waited in the jeep as Major Mills led Mason toward the Tomato Defense Planning Area. "We've had some setbacks during the night," said Major

Mills.

"Serious ones?"

"Well, how many states do you have relatives in?"

"I'm not sure," said Mason. "Three or four."

"Not anymore."

"It's really that bad?"

"I don't like to throw the word 'apocalyptic hellscape' around willy-nilly, but we're getting close. Remember Arkansas?"

"Yes."

"Cherish those memories, because you won't be making any new ones. Have you settled all of your business in Delaware? I sure hope so, because now it's more like Tomatoaware. Or Delamato. Sorry—the word "tomato" doesn't really blend with state names very well, despite the efforts of our top linguists."

They entered the planning area. The walls were covered with maps, along with a poster of the "Hang In There!" kitten that had delighted and inspired so many people over the years.

"Major!" said a soldier. "We've lost Tennessee!"

"Did anybody get Bingo on that one?"

"No, but Captain Franks will if we lose West Virginia."

"Well, let's try to keep that from happening."

"It looks like the entire nation has been taken over by tomatoes!" said Mason. "How did things get so bad so quickly?"

"Nobody knows," said Major Mills. "The top theory is 'inaction,' but honestly, nobody knows."

"What can we do?"

"One option is that we can simply accept our inevitable doom and revert to feral hedonism. Can you imagine how much larceny you could commit if you didn't have to worry about the consequences?"

"What's another option?" asked Mason.

"Allow the horror to completely envelop our minds. The tomatoes won't seem so scary if we're comatose."

"Not a fan of that one, either."

"There is a third option. Prime intelligence tells us that the tomatoes are amassing for a final all-out attack on the nation. Our top brass wants us to concentrate our forces on the West Coast. If we can hold them there, we can win."

"I'm no military strategist," said Mason. "But if the tomatoes have conquered almost the entire nation, why would they congregate on the West Coast and give us one final opportunity to defeat them?"

"It's easy to lose sight of this amidst all of the death and destruction, but remember, they're still tomatoes."

"True. So is that the option we're going with? Holding them at the West Coast?"

"It *wasn't*, but now that we've had this conversation I'm starting to see the merits. Good talk, Dixon."

————

Mason and Finletter parked the jeep and walked back toward their hotel. In retrospect, Mason realized that he could have parked closer, perhaps even in the hotel's parking lot, but he had a lot on his mind.

A gunshot rang out.

"Again?" asked Mason.

He and Finletter looked around. There was a man in a black mask pointing a gun in their direction. They glanced around to see who he might be pointing the gun at, but there was nobody else in the general vicinity. He was pointing the gun at *them!*

There are times when a man must decide if he is going to face danger with bravery, or if he is going to be a coward. Mason had decided long ago that it would be the latter. He fled.

The man fired at Finletter, hitting him right in the parachute. Then he turned and ran.

Finletter chased after him.

They ran through a park. The shadow of the camera crew could briefly be seen on Finletter's parachute, but it was trailing behind him so he didn't notice.

Oh, it was a wild chase! You should've seen it. There was this one part where they ran on top of a parked car, and another part where they climbed over these wooden crates! One tragic omission was that the gunman never said, "Feets, don't fail me now!" but it can be forgiven.

They ran and ran and ran. It's making me tired to even describe it. As an author, the only exercise I get is walking to and from the refrigerator, and whining about bad reviews. (But not for *this* book, which will be a critical darling!)

Finletter had practiced what noise he would make if the wind caught his parachute while he was running. It would be sort of an "Urp!" sound before he was carried off. But it didn't happen.

Finletter was gaining on the gunman. The gunman ran across some train tracks, but then, in a completely unexpected move, turned around and pointed his gun at Finletter.

Finletter stopped running and put his hands in the air.

There was no escape.

This was the end. The man was going to shoot him, and he'd be dead, just like the people who'd been eaten by tomatoes. Finletter did not fear death. He knew that, overall, he'd been a decent human being and was confident that he'd be reincarnated as a gazelle. Of course, he'd be reincarnated as a gazelle in a world overrun by killer tomatoes, so he'd probably die again a few minutes later, but still...

A train sped by, separating the two men.

This was Finletter's chance to escape. But it seemed kind of unfair to the gunman to have his opportunity taken away by a train. If you looked at it from his perspective, he'd been just about to vanquish his foe, when a train messed everything up through no fault of his own. The gunman had no say over the train schedule. One moment he was victorious, and the next moment it was snatched away. That wasn't right.

Finletter didn't want to escape like this. It was like when he'd been in wrestling in high school and his opponent twisted his ankle right before the match. Finletter won by default. It wasn't any fun. He couldn't celebrate the win.

He stood there, hands in the air, waiting for the train to pass. Fortunately, there were plenty of interesting logos on the side of the train cars to keep him entertained as he waited.

When the train finally passed, the gunman was gone.

Finletter slowly lowered his hands.

Wow. The gunman had been raptured.

———

"So you can see, Mr. Dixon," said President Griffin, over the phone, "we have no choice but to make our stand out west. And I need you out there with our military people, to make sure they understand the enormity of their responsibility. If there's one thing I know about the military, it's that they appreciate feedback from civilians."

"I understand, Mr. President. How's the ad campaign going?"

"Excellent. The latest polls show that 53% of Americans are rooting for us to defeat the tomatoes."

"That's excellent?"

"In this country? Absolutely."

"Before we hang up," said Mason, "can I ask about Project: Proactive?"

"Ah, yes. Came up with it myself. It's where we proactively bomb cities that haven't been overtaken by the tomatoes yet, cutting off their food source. It's based on the theory that if there's not a win/win situation, a lose/lose is the next best thing."

"Now that you've explained it, I withdraw my objection."

CHAPTER 16

Sam Smith was having a better time hanging out with the tomatoes than he would've expected. They had plenty of entertaining anecdotes to share, and Sam couldn't deny that human flesh was quite tasty when cooked properly. He wouldn't kill anybody for food when this was over, obviously, but there was no lack of dead bodies lying around, free for the taking, and he might gather some to store in his freezer.

One of the tomatoes finished a hilarious story about slurping out somebody's eyeballs, and Sam and the other tomatoes laughed and laughed and laughed. Somebody handed Sam an arm, and though he was full, there was no reason he couldn't gnaw on it a bit.

He took a bite. The arm was overcooked.

"Could somebody pass the ketchup?" he asked.

The tomatoes went silent. Sam realized his horrifying mistake but tried to remain calm.

"Ha ha," said Sam. "That was an amusing joke."

The tomatoes did not seem amused.

"Imagine, a tomato putting ketchup on their food! I sure wouldn't want to sit around the campfire with *that* particular tomato, that's for sure!" Sam laughed to show how funny it was. "Ketchup. Tee hee!"

The tomatoes continued to sit there. Silent. Motionless.

"Okay, I'm going to level with you," said Sam. "I'm not a real tomato. I'm a traitor to humankind. I saw you guys eating people and I thought, 'I like their style. How can I get in on that action?' So I fashioned this tomato costume, made with nothing but love and admiration, and then I decided to join you to help plot how we can bring an end to the human race. Die, filthy humans, die! Long live the tomato overlords!"

You lied to us, said one of the tomatoes.

"It wasn't a lie," said Sam. "I withheld information."

We trusted you. This betrayal stings. How can we ever learn to trust anybody again after what you've done?

"Don't be that way. Yes, I tried to deceive you, but my heart was in the right place. You can't let this affect the way you feel about other people. Don't close yourself off."

Perhaps you're right.

"Anyway, I've taken up enough of your time," said Sam, standing up. "I'll be on my way now. Thank you for the yummy body parts."

Wait. We will give you a chance to prove your loyalty.

Sam hesitated.

Two tomatoes brought out a young woman. Her hands were bound behind her back with vines.

Kill her, the tomato told Sam.

The woman shook her head. "Please! Please, no! Don't hurt me! I'll do anything!"

Kill her! Kill her now! Kill her with your teeth!

"I...I...I'm not hungry," said Sam.

This isn't about hunger! We'll eat the leftovers! Prove your loyalty and end her accursed life, human!

Sam walked over to the sobbing woman. He opened his mouth.

"I'm sorry," he told her. "I'm so very, very sorry."

"Please!" she begged. "I have a family! My children depend on me!"

Sam leaned his mouth closer to her neck.

"They must be so worried! Darla is only two! Please don't make Darla grow up without a mother! My husband has that parenting style where he's more like a friend than a father and he leaves all of the disciplining up to me! Darla will be disrespectful to authority figures if I'm not there to raise her right! Please!"

Sam closed his mouth and stepped away. Then he opened his mouth again, but only to speak. "I can't do it."

Then you shall die!

"You'll have to catch me first!" he shouted, as he turned and ran away.

He heard the woman's agonized wail behind him as he fled.

Did this still count as a moral victory if he left her behind to die? Maybe taking a bite out of her throat would've been granting her mercy.

He couldn't do this. He couldn't run away. It would be a total douchebag move.

He had to return to the campfire and rescue her. Yes, thousands, perhaps millions, of people had been killed by the tomatoes, so in the grand scheme of things he wasn't contributing much to humanity by saving one person. Still, he had to do it.

He ran back to the campfire. The tomatoes attacked.

It was one man against fifty tomatoes. He didn't stand a chance.

As the tomatoes swarmed him, Sam regretted

coming back to try to save the woman. Yes, he'd have felt guilty leaving her behind to perish, but at least he could've felt that guilt while being alive.

His tomato costume would protect him for a couple of minutes, even though he didn't plan to spend those minutes in a particularly productive manner. Screaming, mostly.

So much senseless mayhem surrounded him. Though Sam used to believe that man was the cruelest beast of them all, he now knew that it was tomatoes. Their bloodlust knew no bounds.

But Sam started to realize that, although there was tomato violence happening all around him, he was not currently being killed. What was happening?

His disguise! It was too convincing! The tomatoes didn't know which one he was! They were attacking each other instead of the stranger in their midst!

As the tomatoes battled each other in confusion, Sam saw an opportunity to escape. The woman saw it, too, and she grabbed his hand. Together they ran away from the campfire, leaving the tomatoes behind.

"My name is Tiffany," the woman said.

"I'm Sam Smith, disguise expert." He unzipped his costume and let the cloth tomato suit fall to the ground.

"Thank you for not biting out my throat under duress."

"You're welcome. Now you've been given a second chance. Go back to your husband and children, and live life to the fullest."

"Oh, I made them up so you wouldn't kill me. I'm single. And available. And ready to live life to the fullest, if you know what I mean."

"Ah," said Sam. "I'm not sure I appreciate being lied to."

"You just lied about being a tomato."

"Right. I recognize the irony. But humans have double standards. It's what separates us from the vegetables."

Tiffany nodded. "I understand."

"But I hope you find happiness."

"And I hope you do, too."

They parted ways. Ultimately, both of them would find happiness, but they'd also always wonder what might have been.

———

Another military base.

"The men look ready, Major," said Mason. He wasn't exactly sure what constituted "ready," but he saw them waving lots of guns around and nobody was currently weeping in the fetal position, so he assumed they were prepared for the final tomato onslaught.

Major Mills nodded. "You know, Dixon. A man stops to think at a time like this."

"He sure does," said Finletter. "So much stopping. So much thinking."

"About his home," Mills continued. "His wife. His kids. And how he has none of these and how nobody will miss him if he was to die tonight. The fact that he has nothing to live for and, thus, doesn't care whether he lives or dies factors into the decisions he makes in battle. Grim stuff, gentlemen. Grim stuff."

"I wonder what the tomatoes are thinking right now?" asked Finletter.

"Who knows what goes on in the mind of a tomato? They can't be normal thoughts. I suspect that if we could spend just one moment in their mind we'd be driven completely mad. Would we be screaming forever, unable to stop, or would it be the quiet kind of madness? There's no way to know. All I can say is that the mind of a tomato is dark and disturbing, and we should thank the heavens every hour on the hour that we don't have to experience it for ourselves."

"Or maybe they don't think about much of anything," said Mason.

"Please don't contradict my theory in front of your assistant," said Mills.

A soldier gave Mills a thumbs-up.

Mills returned the gesture. "That's the signal. They're ready for their musical number."

"They're doing a musical number?"

"Of course they're doing a musical number. You can't go off to war without one. Soldiers should die with a song in their heart."

The soldiers lined up. The lead singer took a step forward, and a spotlight shone on him. Dramatic music began to play, its source unknown.

"We stopped the Germans in '45."

He had a lovely voice. Mason was glad there'd be this moment of beautiful music before the gorefest.

"Then we crushed the Viet Cong."

"Almost," the backup singers added.

"For a greater glory we could never strive. This crop uprising won't last long."

"Long doesn't rhyme very well with *strive,"* Finletter whispered. "Should we say something?"

"That's not the rhyming pattern they're using," Mason whispered back. *"Strive* rhymes with *'45. Cong* rhymes with *long."*

"You're right. My fault. Sorry."

The music changed, becoming way more uptempo. The lead singer removed his helmet, flung it away with flourish, and then began to dance. No doubt about it—he knew how to sway those hips.

"*Ain't no time to make a fuss. We got to get these toma-toes before they get us.*"

Other soldiers joined in. "*We're gonna beat 'em, mash 'em, squish 'em, bash 'em in the street. We're gonna kick 'em, kick 'em, mush 'em, crush 'em with our feet.*"

Soldiers began to shoot off heavy artillery in time with the music.

"*T-O-M-A-T-O-E-S!*" they sang. There was a brief pause while everybody confirmed that this was the correct spelling, and then the song resumed.

"*We'll squish them! We'll mash them! We'll mush them! We'll crush them!*"

Mason had to admit that the musical number was really inspiring him. He was no soldier, but he was ready to go pick up the helmet that the lead singer had tossed aside and rush straight into battle.

"*We stopped to negotiate at the first attack. We gave 'em Alabama but they gave it right back.*"

(Note: If you are from Alabama, or have a fond-ness for the state, feel free to replace that lyric with "California," or any state of your choosing.)

"*Tomatoes!*" sang the lead singer.

"*Tomatoes!*" sang the backup singers.

"*Tomatoes!*" sang the lead singer.

"*Tomatoes!*" sang the backup singers.

"*Tomatoes!*" sang the lead singer.

"*Tomatoes!*" sang the backup singers.

(Remember, it's perfectly fine to sing and dance along to this book. Get that body in motion! Dance like nobody's watching, even though they totally are, and judging you. Wave your hands in the air like you just don't care—by which I mean lethargically.)

"*They said we'd live together like sister and brother. But they captured a cannery and bottled my mother. Now she's at the store and they'll soon be back for more. Those tomatoes!*"

Overhead, planes flew in zigzag patterns in time to the music.

Many of 1978's most popular musical acts, including the Bee Gees and ABBA, joined in.

"Tomatoes!" sang the backup singers.

Cannons went off to provide a big finish.

"Those tomatoes!" sang the lead singer.

Everybody cheered and applauded. Morale was high. Mason was beginning to believe that they would actually win this war.

CHAPTER 17

At the stroke of midnight, the tomatoes attacked.

The musical number, and many others like it, had inspired our men and women in uniform to fight their hardest against the tomato menace. But the songs in their heart were quickly replaced by screams in their mouths.

As the tanks rolled forward, the night was filled with the sounds of gunfire, hand grenades, bombs, and people going "AAAHHH!!!" And, of course, the maddening, incessant babbling of the tomatoes. Happy sounds from humans were few and far between.

———

Private #1 was on the front lines of the battle, so he knew he was going to die, but he was surprised by how quickly it happened.

———

Privates #2 and #3 fired lots and lots of bullets at the tomatoes. They were both very good at shooting, and the overwhelming majority of their bullets made their way into tomatoes. The problem was that one bullet wasn't enough to finish off a giant killer tomato—it took sixty-seven bullets per tomato to make it stop trying to eat people, and even with plenty of practice, it was difficult to shoot the same tomato sixty-seven times.

It also didn't help that, as far as they could tell, they were facing about a trillion gazillion tomatoes.

"It's been an honor serving with you," said Private #2, about thirty seconds too late. But maybe Private #3 could hear him from inside the tomato.

"It's been an honor serving with you as well," said Private #4, thinking Private #2 had been talking to him. Private #2 didn't bother to correct him. Why make things awkward?

Soon, Privates #2 through #89 had fallen. Which we can all agree is bad enough, but plenty more would perish before this dark, dark night was over.

Private #90 drove forward in his tank. He'd spent most of his military career complaining that tanks moved too slowly (he lost every race), but right now, as soldiers died all around him, he was happy for the protection.

"Boy, I sure am glad we're in a tank," said his co-pilot, Private #361. (It was an imperfect numbering system.) "Can you imagine being one of those poor suckers who's not in a tank right now? It really makes you appreciate the little things, like being in a tank."

"There's a tomato up ahead," said Private #90.

"I'm on it." Private #361 spun the cannon turret around and fired. "Whoopsie."

"Not your best shot."

"No, it sure wasn't. What I like best about being in a tank is if we were outside, we'd have to apologize for blowing away a few of our own men, but here we can just carry on as if nothing happened. It's like the walls of this tank shield us from danger, and also consequences."

"True, but the tomato is still there."

"It's not distracted by eating the soldiers we just killed?"

"Nope."

Private #361 fired again. "Oooh. Another blunder. You know what? I'm just going to come right out and say it: Aim isn't my strong suit. I'm pretty good at spinning the turret but not so great at figuring out where to stop." He fired once more. "Wow. Zero for three. You'd think that by now a tomato would've rolled into the spot where I was shooting, just by accident."

Something heavy struck the tank.

"Felt like you crashed into something," said Private #361. "Try to steer a little more carefully in the future."

"I think we got hit by a tomato!" Something else struck the tank. "They're attacking us!"

"They can't be! Don't they know we're in a tank?"

"Start shooting in blind panic! Start shooting in blind panic!"

Both soldiers screamed as the tank toppled over onto its side. This was insanity! Tomatoes, even oversized ones in large numbers, couldn't overturn a tank, could they?

"Our periscope has been damaged!" said Private

#90. "If we want to know what's going on outside, we'll have to open the hatch!"

"Don't do it! The hatch is the only thing protecting us from the tomatoes and our angry fellow soldiers!"

The hatch opened, but not because Private #90 had ignored Private #361's advice. Somebody else had opened it. Private #90 desperately hoped that it was another soldier, because the idea that tomatoes could open the hatch of a tank was too terrifying to bear.

What had opened the hatch? They would never know. And nothing is more frightening than ambiguity.

———

Actually, that's not true. Getting eaten by giant tomatoes is more frightening than ambiguity. Yes, the tomatoes got the hatch open, and then they squeezed through the opening because tomatoes have no bones, and then they ate both privates.

Fortunately, the tank was beyond repair, because the only thing more frightening than ambiguity and getting eaten by tomatoes is the idea of tomatoes driving tanks.

———

Explosions everywhere.

"Starts to hurt your ears after a while, doesn't it?" asked Private #938.

"What's that?" asked Private #700.

"I said, it starts to hurt your ears after a while, doesn't it?"

"Oh, sorry. I couldn't hear you because I was wearing Zapper brand ear plugs. They're the perfect ear plugs for rock concerts, noisy neighbors, and war."

"But what makes Zapper ear plugs better than the leading brand?"

"Only Zapper brand ear plugs are guaranteed to protect you from slugs slithering into your ear canal. If you're using another brand, why, you might as well dangle a sign from your earlobe saying 'Welcome, Slugs!'"

"Well, I'm convinced!" said Private #938. "I'm going to buy a pair of Zapper brand ear plugs right now!"

"No, you're not," said Private #700. "We're currently in the midst of a fierce battle with the giant killer tomatoes. We'll be lucky to survive the night. You had plenty of time to buy them beforehand. Did you think there'd be no explosions?"

Private #700, distracted by the conversation, didn't notice the tomato sneaking up behind him. He shrieked as the tomato gobbled him up. Soon all that was left of him was his ears.

Though this seemed like an ironic opportunity for Private #938, he was being eaten by a different tomato at the same time, and the ear plugs went to waste.

———

Major Mills realized that he was cornered by a tomato.

"No!" he shouted. "You can't do this! I'm one of the characters that the reader has grown the most attached to! I may not be Mason Dixon or Lieutenant Finletter or Jim Richardson or Lois Fairchild, but I'm at least the fifth-most important character! You can't kill off the fifth-most important character in a book! The readers won't stand for it!"

The tomato didn't care what the readers thought, and that was the end of Major Mills.

———

Captain Marcus Bridgeforth III had come out of retirement just to battle the tomatoes. He was ninety-two years old, but looked and moved like a much older man, so he contributed very little to the offensive effort. Still, the other soldiers recognized that his heart was in the right place, and they were disappointed when a tomato rolled right over him, squishing him flat.

———

One battalion of soldiers had come up with the idea that though the tomatoes wanted to bring about the extinction of humankind, they might not be so hostile toward other vegetables. So each of the eight hundred soldiers were armed with carrots, celery, turnips, radishes, etc. that had been carved into sharp points.

"Attack!" the Lieutenant Colonel shouted.

At first it worked. The tomatoes, reluctant to attack other plant life, hesitated just long enough to give the soldiers an advantage. Carrots plunged into tomatoes like daggers. Soon the battlefield was littered with dead and dying hole-covered tomatoes. Their death babbles were a haunting symphony.

But their numbers were just too great. For every tomato that died, two more took its place.

"A battalion isn't enough!" the Lieutenant Colonel declared. "We need a brigade! A division! A corps! A field army!"

"A field army?" asked a random soldier standing in the area. "That's more than fifty thousand soldiers!

We could never pay that many extras! It's impossible!"

"Not in the movie version, no! For the movie, we're lucky it wasn't just the same two actors running back and forth. But this is a book! It's the cinema of the mind! We're limited only by the author's imagination!"

"Then we're screwed," said the soldier.

"Wrong! There they are!"

And there they were. Fifty thousand soldiers. Each of them wearing uniforms with flawless attention to detail. All of them stunningly handsome—leading men, not character actors.

They all had sharpened vegetables.

Not just carrots and celery. Exotic vegetables like Romanesco and Kohlrabi.

"Chaaaaaaarge!" shouted the Lieutenant Colonel.

"Whoa, whoa, whoa," said the random soldier. "Lieutenant Colonels don't command field armies. Do you want readers to think we didn't do any research?"

"Chaaaaaaarge!" shouted a four-star general.

Fifty thousand soldiers rushed forward. The tomatoes didn't stand a chance.

Or did they?

The soldiers stabbed and stabbed. The tomatoes, being one of the more liquidy vegetables, sprayed juice everywhere as the soldiers fought as if they were humanity's last stand. Soldiers were so drenched in tomato slime that their bodies glistened in the moonlight, and in some places the slime was so deep that the soldiers trudged forth as if moving through a wading pool.

"Does it bother anybody else that we're wasting food?" asked one of the soldiers.

Tomato after tomato fell dead.

But the sharpened vegetable weapons, which had worked so well in the beginning, began to lose their effectiveness. A sharpened cucumber was only good for a few stabs before the tip broke off, leaving soldiers with a dull cucumber unsuitable for stabbing much of anything. And the tomatoes spread word of the plan to their brethren, warning them that to hesitate was to die.

"It's not working as well anymore!" shouted the general. "Bummer!"

Fifty thousand soldiers became forty thousand.

Forty thousand soldiers became thirty thousand.

"Cast away your vegetables!" shouted the general. "We still have guns!"

The soldiers opened fire. Tomatoes continued to splatter.

Yet there were still too many of them.

Thirty thousand soldiers became twenty thousand.

Twenty thousand soldiers became ten thousand.

"Technically, we're a division now," said a two-star major general. "I think you'll find that my management style differs a bit from my predecessor. Violence has its place, but maybe we should try being nice to the tomatoes for a while. It can't hurt, right?"

Ten thousand soldiers became eight thousand.

Eight thousand soldiers became six thousand.

"I would like to apologize to all of you for my lapse in judgment," said the major general. "In retrospect, we should have continued to be violent towards them. It's too late to bring back the soldiers who died as a result of my orders, but let us have a moment of silence for them."

Six thousand soldiers became five thousand.

"Clearly we should have saved the moment of silence for a time when we weren't in immediate danger," said the major general. "Once again, I accept full responsibility. But we're a regiment now, which means that I'll be turning over the leadership role to this brigadier general. Thanks for offering me this opportunity, and I wish you all the best of luck in whatever the future holds."

"I didn't prepare a speech," said the brigadier general. "My leadership style is more of a hands-off approach. You know why we're here: to kill tomatoes. I prefer to trust in your talent and ambition and stay out of your way. If you need me, my door is always open, but I'm not a micro-manager. That said, could somebody check on Private #2938? I think he's having difficulty finding his inhaler."

Five thousand soldiers became four thousand nine hundred and ninety-nine.

The remaining soldiers fought with all of their might, but all across the west coast they were running out of ammunition. They tried beating the tomatoes with their empty guns, which actually worked pretty well. Yet there were still too many tomatoes.

The number of soldiers continued to dwindle.

And dwindle. And dwindle.

"I don't mean to take away from the gravity of the situation," said the brigadier general, "but 'dwindle' sure is a funny word, isn't it? Dwindle."

The battle raged on throughout the night, but it was looking pretty bad for humanity.

Would the tomatoes win? Were we all doomed?

Keep reading to find out!

INTERMISSION

Take this time for a few minutes of silent reflection about what you've read. What have you learned? How has your world view changed? Given the chance to do it all over, knowing what you know now, would you choose to read a different book instead?

CHAPTER 18

INTERMISSION

"How's the ol' war going?" asked President Griffin.

Mason was perspiring so heavily that it was difficult to hold the phone. "Not well. Not well at all. An
almost unimaginable number of casualties."

"You mean on our side?"

"Yes, Mr. President."

"Damn. I was feeling good there for a moment."

"I did say that it wasn't going well at all."

"Right, right. That you did. I just wasn't sure
which side you were referring to. It certainly
wouldn't be going well for the tomatoes if they had
an almost unimaginable number of casualties."

"That's true, Mr. President."

"Have you ever thought about how silly it is that
people are supposed to address me as 'Mr. President'?
I feel like at some point somebody got nervous and
just blurted that out, and then it stuck because nobody wanted to say anything. 'Mr. President.' You see
it too, right?"

"What would you have chosen instead?" Mason
asked.

"Nothing too arrogant. Maybe 'My President.' Obviously, as Americans are getting wiped out by the thousands there are more important things for us to discuss, but this has been bugging me for a while."

"I understand."

"So, we're all gonna die, huh?"

———

Colonel Zinc's tone was somber as he addressed the dozen pilots. "Your planes have been loaded with explosives, and the time of your departure is nigh. It is a tremendous, selfless, noble thing that you do for your country, and your sacrifice will never be forgotten."

The pilots were silent, lost in thought.

Colonel Zinc shook each of their hands in turn and thanked them. "And now, it is time to board your aircrafts, and play your crucial role in eradicating the tomato threat."

Pilot Franklin nodded. "And I look forward to grabbing a beer with everybody when this is over."

"Excuse me?" asked Colonel Zinc.

"You know, to celebrate our victory."

"Well, uh, you won't be returning. None of you will."

"Oh. Where were we supposed to go afterward?"

"Your mission is to crash your explosive-filled planes into highly concentrated groups of tomatoes."

"Right. I got that part."

"You will be in the planes when they explode."

"*Oh.* Okay. That went right over my head. Now I get why everybody is so glum."

"The time has come," said Colonel Zinc. "Once again, your sacrifice will never be forgotten."

Pilot Franklin raised his hand. "Are our vests in the planes?"

"What vests?"

"The vests to protect us from the explosions."

"No, no, no," said Colonel Zinc. "You're not understanding how this works. Your entire plane is going to blow up."

"Oh. So it's a full suit instead of a vest?"

"No. You're not going to survive. None of you are."

Pilot Franklin narrowed his eyes. "This sounds like a suicide mission."

"Yes! That's exactly what it is!"

"Who would do a silly thing like that?"

"Pilots who are willing to sacrifice themselves to ensure the survival of the human race!"

"But we wouldn't be around to enjoy it."

"I know! That's why it's a sacrifice!"

"Couldn't we just jump out of the plane right before it hits?"

"The idea is that you're crashing into the targets with precision. If you jump out of the plane before it hits, it might miss."

"Yeah, you're right. Planes don't steer themselves very well."

"Are we clear on how this is going to work?"

Pilot Franklin nodded.

"So, again, gentlemen, the time has come. Board your planes and know that you have the respect and admiration of the entire country."

"And the first round is on me," said Pilot Jones.

"Wait, what?" asked Colonel Zinc. "What did we just discuss?"

"Is this still a suicide mission?"

"Yes!"

"Oh. I thought it was one of those deals where you say it out loud and then realize how ridiculous it is."

"It's not ridiculous!"

"Are *you* going?"

"No."

"Oh, gee, what a surprise!"

Colonel Zinc began to angrily pace in front of the pilots. "Look, nobody is making you do this. You all volunteered. It said right there on the sign-up sheet: *Kamikaze pilots needed.*"

"I can speak to that," said Pilot Black. "I didn't know what 'kamikaze' meant. It sounded fun and exotic."

The other pilots murmured their agreement.

Pilot Franklin raised his hand. "What if we—hear me out—dropped explosives on the tomatoes but didn't purposely crash the planes into them? That would work, right? I assume these planes were intended for more than one use."

"We have other pilots dropping bombs on the tomatoes at this very moment," said Colonel Zinc. "The whole idea was that you were going to do extra bonus damage. Surely one of you understands the importance of this mission and is willing to sacrifice himself for the cause!"

"I'll do it," said Pilot Black.

"Thank you!"

"But you have to buy me a beer afterward."

Colonel Zinc took his own life out of sheer frustration, and only a couple of the pilots recognized the irony.

———

Private Corker pulled the pin out of a hand grenade and flung it at the nearest tomato. The grenade exploded, sending tomato chunks flying into the air. "Ha! That'll teach you to eat humans!"

"*Not*," said Private Tumbler.

"What?"

"It taught the tomato *not* to eat humans."

"Oh, wow. I've been saying it wrong all this time."

"It's okay. Plenty of people do."

Private Corker flung another hand grenade, blowing the stem off the top of a tomato. "Ha! That'll teach you not to eat humans!" He frowned. "That sounds wrong."

"It's correct, though."

"I know. But it just sounds weird to say it like that. Throwing hand grenades and mocking tomatoes is supposed to be exhilarating, but now I'm all self-conscious."

"I guess I shouldn't have said anything," said Private Tumbler.

"Yeah, honestly, I wish you hadn't."

"Look, if you want to go back to the way you were saying it, that's fine with me. We're responsible for each other's lives, not our grammar."

"Nah. That was my last grenade. And we're surrounded. I'm not trying to throw a guilt trip on you, but the last words I'll ever hear were criticism."

"Sorry."

————

Private Beller was trapped in an alley between two tomatoes. They rolled closer and closer.

"Just leave me be!" he shouted. "I never ate your kind! I was a total carnivore—one of those obnoxious ones who is always making fun of vegetarians! The only toppings I ever put on my burgers were more meat! I'm not your enemy!"

The tomatoes collided, squashing Private Beller between them.

Now he looks like a hamburger patty.

Ha ha. Good one.

"Let's roast these here tomaters!" shouted Private Danker, letting loose with his flamethrower. A giant tomato rolled away, charred and smelling delicious.

He blasted tomato after tomato with the flames. This was how the Americans would win.

———

"Holy cow!" screamed Private Waller. "Flaming tomatoes!"

The burning tomatoes rolled toward them like something out of Hell. The soldiers dropped their weapons and fled.

Soon the entire west coast was aflame.

———

"We're losing horribly," Mason told the president. "Fires everywhere! And the fire engines keep getting attacked by tomatoes! It's absolute pandemonium!"

"What about lakes?" asked President Griffin. "Those have water, right? Send some helicopters with giant buckets over there immediately!"

"Yes, My President!"

———

You know the urban legend about the forest fire and the scuba diver?

One minute, Greg Colburn, underwater expert, was swimming around in a lake, minding his own business. The next, he was in a massive bucket of lake water, being carried away by a helicopter.

"Help! Help me!" he cried out, though nobody

could hear him because he was underwater, speaking through a snorkel, and because helicopters are quite loud.

The helicopter dumped the water on a burning section of the forest. It extinguished the flames...and it also extinguished Greg Colburn.

Totally true. A friend of a friend told me.

———

Back where the musical number began, the soldiers did a very downbeat reprise of "Tomato Stomp."

———

The fighting continued throughout the night. Yes, a great many tomatoes were obliterated, but the loss of human life was much greater. If this was to be mankind's final stand, well, mankind had botched the job.

A few remaining soldiers hid in a foxhole. "Remember when it was just that one housewife getting killed by a single tomato while doing the dishes?" one asked. "Such an innocent time."

"Yeah," said another soldier. "I think we're all nostalgic for when it was just the occasional lighthearted death, instead of this nihilistic nightmare."

"I guess it could be worse, though," said the first soldier.

"How?"

"I'm not sure. But we're only about three-fifths of the way into the book, so there's plenty of time to escalate."

"Aw, crap. I thought things were wrapping up."

"Oh, no. There's carnage galore on the way."

The soldiers began to cry. Then they realized that

there was a great big tomato in the foxhole with them, and their fond reminisces of happier times came to a gruesome end.

————

As the sun rose, the tomatoes rolled away from the battlefields, victorious.

Did they mourn their dead? Nobody knows. You'd have to ask them.

In the battle of Human Vs. Tomato, the humans got their butts kicked into oblivion. The remaining humans staggered through the empty streets, shielding their eyes from the painful sunlight, wondering if the world would ever return to normal.

CHAPTER 19

Across the nation, the tomatoes continued on their rampage of wanton destruction.

Last night's crushing military defeat might have spelled the end of humanity. The shattered remnants of a once-proud civilization lay scattered amongst crushed spirits and broken bodies.

Mason walked through the hellscape of what had once been a perfectly nice city. A reporter interviewed one of the survivors.

"Across this great nation," the reporter said into the camera, "almost everyone has been affected in one way or another by this terrible tomato onslaught. Mrs. Williams, I understand that your husband is missing."

"Yes, he is."

"Do you think he's one of the lucky ones who died quickly?"

"I—"

"Is it possible that he's seriously injured? Perhaps lying in a ditch with two broken legs, crying out your name, as you stand here giving an interview to a stranger?"

"I—"

"Will you have dinner with me, Mrs. Williams?"

"No!"

"I understand that asking you on a date was inappropriate, but don't you agree that it's time to let go of the old standards of behavior? These are the After Times, and social norms no longer apply. Obviously I don't mean that I'm going to hit you over the head with a wooden club and drag you off to my cave—we're not there quite yet—but waiting for confirmation of your husband's death feels like an unnecessary hurdle."

"May I leave now?"

"No, Mrs. Williams, you may not. What if, hypothetically, your husband returns, but because of the things he's witnessed he's a mere shell of his former self? Could you still love a man without the ability to experience joy?"

"This interview is over!"

"Oh, no, it most definitely isn't. These guns aren't just for show."

Mason continued unhappily on his way. The streets were barren. Occasionally somebody peeked through the corner of a broken window, but they disappeared as soon as Mason looked in their direction.

He noticed a small splotch of tomato juice on the sidewalk. No, it was a whole trail of splotches, as if an injured tomato had rolled this way.

Stomping on an injured tomato would make Mason feel a lot better. He loathed what he had become, but couldn't deny the urge within.

He followed the trail through an alley, stepping over a few bodies on the way, until he finally found the cornered tomato. It trembled in fear as he raised his foot over it, relishing the thought of how it would burst apart under his shoe.

And yet something didn't feel right.

Was it really trembling in fear? Or was it trembling in...laughter?

There were no signs of injury! The tomato had smeared itself with the juice of another! It was a trap!

Several more tomatoes rolled out of their hiding spots, babbling with glee.

Mason ran.

The tomatoes followed.

They chased him out of the alley and down the sidewalk. They were moving incredibly fast, as if somebody off-camera had hurled them at a very high velocity.

Mason hurried up some stone steps. The tomatoes followed.

He raced around a corner. Thanks to the magic of clever editing, the tomatoes followed.

He ran through an apartment complex. He threw open the nearest door and went inside, hoping he wouldn't be putting any innocent people in danger. The woman inside gasped and almost dropped her two babies.

The tomatoes rolled into the apartment. Mason wondered if they knew that baby meat was the sweetest meat of them all.

A commercial was playing on the radio. *"You got chocolate in my peanut butter!"* somebody said.

"You got peanut butter in my chocolate!"

"I'm going to sue, you son of a bitch!"

The announcer spoke over the sounds of a scuffle. *"Have you been in an accident that ruined the snack you were enjoying? The law offices of Wilbur, Hertzfeld, Tamale, Gorgenmeyer, Rassenberg, Ignasius, and Spitz will get you the justice you seek!"*

The tomatoes rolled closer.

"I don't know which child to feed it first!" the woman wailed.

"Hey, it's time to get back to the music," said the dee-jay. "Next up, it's the song that brings a speck of happiness to our lives in these dark apocalyptic times!"

Puberty.
Puberty love.
Puberty.
Puberty love.
Puberty.
Puberty love.

The tomatoes rolled out of the apartment.

"That's strange," said Mason. "They forgot to kill us."

The woman hugged her babies to her chest. "I'm glad I get to keep both of them, though I won't lie, a lot of anguish went into the decision for nothing."

Mason waited for a few minutes, then stepped out of the apartment. The tomatoes were gone.

How very, very quaint. If only there was some sort of consistent element involved. They must have left for *some* reason, but what could it have been? Had he made a particular facial expression that scared them off?

As he returned to his car, he gasped in shock. The man in the facemask, the one who'd tried to shoot him, had the front hood open and was messing with Mason's car. You didn't mess with another man's automobile!

Finletter sat in the driver's seat, fast asleep. Mason had *told* him to take a nap earlier, and now look what happened.

"Hey!" Mason shouted.

The man in the facemask hurried to his own car, got in, and started the engine.

After the last chase sequence, Mason had started

carrying a gun. He took it out and fired a pair of warning shots into the sky. But the gun was heavier than he'd anticipated, and the shots actually went into the masked man's rear tires. His car very slowly moved forward.

The gunshots awoke Finletter, who immediately started the engine. But thanks to the sabotage, the car barely moved.

"He's getting away!" Mason said. "We have to push!"

Finletter got out of the car and helped Mason push the vehicle after the masked man's car. It was a frenzied chase, but nearly five feet separated the two cars, and Mason was unable to close the gap.

"The road slopes downward up ahead!" said Finletter. "We might be able to build up some momentum and catch him!"

"But he'll be going downhill, too!" said Mason.

"Argh!"

"Push harder! We can't let him get away!" A moment later, Mason said, "I'm getting tired. How long can we possibly keep up this four-miles-per-hour pace?"

"Don't give up!" said Finletter. "It'll be worth it when we get to torture him!"

"No torture!"

"We're gaining on him! Stay motivated!"

Mason began to push his car with renewed enthusiasm. And then it happened. The two cars collided with a loud *plink*.

"Who are you?" Mason shouted at the masked man. "Who do you work for? Answer these questions in order to avoid confusion!"

The masked man said nothing. Instead, he pointed a gun at them.

Mason cursed himself for purchasing a revolver that only held two bullets.

"Don't worry," said Finletter. "A train will come by any moment now."

"We're not anywhere close to train tracks."

Finletter glanced around. "Well, that's disappointing."

"Knock yourselves unconscious," said the masked man.

"Do you mean that we should knock ourselves unconscious, or that we should knock each other unconscious?" Mason asked.

"However you want to do it."

"Okay. Give us a minute." Mason and Finletter discussed amongst themselves the most efficient way to make this happen, and then knocked each other unconscious.

———

When Mason opened his eyes, a familiar figure sat in front of him.

"*You!*"

CHAPTER 20

Who do YOU think the mystery person is?

Press Secretary Jim Richardson? Surely somebody who works directly for the president couldn't be evil, but you never know...

Journalist Lois Fairchild? Maybe. It would be a pretty big stretch, based on what we've read so far, but there might be a flashback or something that forces you to recontextualize everything.

Lieutenant Finletter? That would be stupid. I'm not saying it *isn't* Finletter, but that would be really frickin' stupid, and I hope it's not.

Major Mills? Just because the book said he was dead, doesn't mean he's really dead. Wouldn't see that twist coming, would you?

Swann from Mind Maker? That's actually better than the real answer. Oh well.

Angus, the psychopath in the library who said "tomato"? That's not out of the question.

The answer will be revealed after this quick word from our sponsor.

ATTACK OF THE KILLER TOMATOES

Do you enjoy ice, but can't stand how cold it always seems to be? Surely there has to be a way for water to be solid without it being so gosh-darn chilly!

Well, now there is! Blocks-o-Water are convenient cubes of solidified water that you can drop into your beverage without the annoyance of them cooling down your drink! No more saying "Brrrr!" when one touches your tongue!

Blocks-o-Water. Solid water without the chill! Available at your local pharmacy.

———————

"Good afternoon, Mr. Dixon," said a familiar voice. "Enjoy your nap?"

"Richardson," said Mason. "I'm not surprised."

(Were YOU surprised? I bet you didn't expect a jaw-dropping plot twist like this in the tomato book, did you?)

"I didn't really think you would be," said Jim. "That's why you're here."

"What do you intend to do with me?"

"Mr. Dixon, don't be so naive. You're the only one with the knowledge that can stop me."

"Oh, I know you're planning to kill me. I was really just asking about the method. There's obviously a big difference between a gun and, say, a circular saw."

"It's funny, Dixon," said Jim. "No man sits closer to power than the Press Secretary to the President of the United States. And yet as close as it is, that power is never really within your grasp. It dangles before you. Taunting you. Daring you. Twerking you while forbidding you to touch it. Mocking your very impotence."

Mason was suddenly very disappointed. He'd assumed all this time that Jim Richardson wasn't completely insane. His lack of sanity was going to make things much more difficult.

"I will not be mocked anymore!" said Jim.

"I will not be mocked anymore!" said Mason, doing his best Jim Richardson impression.

Jim smiled. "I get what you're trying to do. You're trying to enrage me so that I will make a mistake. Very clever."

Actually, Mason was just trying to be a dick, but he didn't argue.

"I will no longer give other people's answers to other people's questions! The answers will be mine! The questions will be mine! Everything will be mine!"

Mason waited politely for him to say "Mine! Mine! Mine!" but Jim didn't take his rant that far.

"It'll be glorious, Dixon. Too bad you won't be around to see it."

"Right," said Mason. "Because of the whole 'you're going to kill me' thing."

"Correct."

"I'll be honest. Right now I don't know anything about your plan except that you're secretly evil."

"Have you had lunch yet?" Jim asked.

"Are you asking for a sinister reason?"

"Perhaps."

"No, I haven't had lunch yet. You're going to offer me a tomato, aren't you?"

"I am." Jim went over to a vegetable basket, picked up a normal-sized tomato, and tossed it to Mason. "Here you go."

"Oh sweet Jesus get it off of me!" Mason screamed. *"Get it off of me! Get it off! Hurry, before it starts eating me! Please, please, I'm begging you, get this monster away from me!"*

Mason stopped screaming as it occurred to him

that the tomato wasn't trying to eat him. It was just a regular tomato.

"Don't be afraid," said Jim. "It's quite harmless."

"Thanks for not telling me that before you threw it at me, jerk."

"It's from my garden."

"So how did you keep it from growing to a giant size and trying to eat people?" asked Mason.

"Let's just say that I'm in...*tune* with my tomatoes."

"Fine. You're in tune with your tomatoes. That's pretty vague. Seriously, how do you control them?"

"Let's just say that...honestly, I don't really have another way of phrasing it. I thought you'd pick it up after the first clue."

"Then what's your master plan? Take over the nation with normal tomatoes?"

"Um, no," said Jim. "I'm going to *save* the nation. At the proper time, when all vestiges of authority have disappeared, I shall charge in on my white stallion and save the United States of America. Or what's left of it."

"Hey, could you take this tomato back?" Mason asked. "I know you said it's harmless and stuff, but I'd feel better if it wasn't on my lap."

"My fellow citizens will be eternally grateful. At the very least, they'll surely choose my benevolent leadership over the obvious alternative."

"Ah, okay. Now I get it. You want to save everybody from the killer tomatoes, excluding the millions that are already dead, and then use your popularity to be elected president. It makes sense, except that you forgot one small detail."

"Which is?"

"You could make *way* more money in the private sector. Think of the endorsement deals. The president makes two hundred grand a year. Not bad, certainly a living wage, but that's nothing compared to the earning potential of a national hero."

"It's not about money," said Jim. "It's about power."

"Same thing. To-may-to, to-mah-to."

"It is *not* the same thing. Do you know how many Americans I've killed? Do you think I'm going to squander my power on a paycheck for hawking toothpaste?"

"Actually, I don't know how many Americans you've killed. How many?"

"Well, none directly."

"I figured that. You don't seem like the kind of guy who gets his hands dirty. I mean, unless you're working in your garden. That's dirty work. Anyway, I guess my question is, did you create the giant killer tomatoes?"

"Oh, no, no," said Jim. "I'm not *that* evil. That's, like, supervillain evil. I'm politician evil."

"Well…"

"Now, now, let's keep the satire toothless. So, no, I did not cause the tomatoes to grow and become homicidal, but I did keep my discovery of how to stop them to myself. It was a perfect plan."

"Was it, though?"

"Yes. Do you think otherwise?"

"I'm not sure you needed to let the tomatoes destroy so much of the country and eat so much of the population. Why not just save a celebrity? Save Burt Reynolds from a giant tomato. That's enough to get a man elected president, I'd think."

"Okay. Yes. That version of the plan has merit," Jim admitted. "But it's too late now, isn't it?"

"I don't know if it's too late to save Burt Reynolds, but thousands of people are being killed by the tomatoes at this very moment. Maybe you should get in tune with them—whatever the hell that means—and save those voters."

"Maybe I will. But there's a loose end to take care of first."

"There's no need to kill me," said Mason. "Yes, I know your whole deranged scheme, but I also know how to keep my mouth shut. I can be a valuable resource. Let me rule by your side."

"Nah." Jim picked up a gun and pointed it at Mason. "I'm afraid, Mr. Dixon, that these are your final moments."

Mason sat up straight. "I don't think you can do it."

"Why would you say something like that?" asked Jim. "Why, when I've got a gun pointed at your face, would you say something that, if I *was* having qualms about killing you, would give me the resolve to do it? It makes no sense as a psychological technique."

"I disagree."

"How can you disagree? 'I don't think you can do it' is a direct attack on my masculinity. Even if I hadn't really planned to shoot you, I would after you said something like that. You're basically double dog daring me to do it. It's a really good way for you to get shot."

"If you say so," said Mason. "I still don't think you can do it."

"Perhaps you're right."

Keeping the gun pointed at Mason, Jim picked up the telephone. "Room service? I'd like a ham sandwich delivered to 503. Thank you."

A few minutes later, there was a knock at the door.

"Come in," said Jim.

The hotel employee opened the door..

Jim shot him in the head.

Mason cried out in shock as the employee fell to the floor, dropping the ham sandwich. Mason might have eaten a sandwich off the floor, but not one that was covered in blood.

"Or," said Jim, "perhaps you're wrong."

"I still don't think you can do it," said Mason.

"Seriously? I just killed that guy."

"Yes, but he was an anonymous victim. Can you murder somebody in cold blood after having a conversation with them?"

"I guess we'll find out," said Jim, pointing the gun at Mason's head. "Do you have any last words?"

"I did, but then you pointed the gun at me, and my mind went blank."

"Then it is time to die."

"Wait!" said Mason.

"What?"

"I remembered my last words."

"Which are...?"

"I'd like to start by reciting my favorite poem, and then transition to the complete works of Mr. Leo Tolstoy."

"Enough of this nonsense," said Jim. "I am now going to squeeze the trigger."

"Wait! Before you kill me, tell me how you were going to defeat the tomatoes. You owe me that much, since you're going to murder me."

"Very well. It's really not that difficult. It harkens back to when I said that I was in *tune* with my tomatoes. The emphasis on the word *tune* was completely intentional. Like many English words, it can have different meanings depending on the context, so what you needed to do was figure out that I was trying to make you think of the noun version of the word, even though that's not how I was using it in that particular sentence. From there—"

Finletter burst into the room and stabbed Jim with his sword.

"Sorry it took me so long," said Finletter. "For a while I was unconscious, and then I woke up in a dark room with my hands and feet tied to a chair. But then I noticed that...oh, wait, hold on, he's not dead yet." Finletter stabbed Jim a few more times. "There we go. Anyway, I noticed that they hadn't....you seem upset, sir. Is it because of your near-death experience?"

"He was going to tell us how to defeat the tomatoes!"

"I thought he was the bad guy."

"He was!"

"I'm confused."

"It doesn't matter."

"Who shot the room service guy?"

"He did."

"Okay, so, then I was right to kill him."

"No!"

"Was the room service guy evil?"

"No!"

"Did you know there's a tomato on your lap?"

"Yes. It's harmless. Jim Richardson figured out how to turn them back into normal tomatoes, but you killed him before he could tell me."

"*Oooohhh.* Okay." Finletter nodded. "Now I get why you're so upset. I was confused for a while. So what do we do?"

Mason stood up. He dropped the tomato onto the floor and then stomped on it.

"There's nothing we can do," he said. "I'm going to call the president and tell him that all is lost."

CHAPTER 21

"That's very disappointing," President Griffin told Mason over the phone. "But I appreciate that you led with the news that we're all going to die. I would've been pretty upset to hear that my press secretary was evil if you'd started there, but in the grand scheme of things, I really don't care."

"There's still a speck of hope," said Mason. "But you know how small a speck is—it's even smaller than a crumb—and I'm ready for you to send me the address of the underground bunker where we'll ride this out."

"What underground bunker?"

"Very amusing, My President, but this is no time for jokes."

"I would never joke about the underground bunker. I mean, I might offer a lighthearted comment like, 'Boy, I sure hope it has a Jacuzzi,' because it would be absurd for an underground bunker to have such a luxury, but I wouldn't joke about its very existence."

"There's no bunker?"

"Why would I squander taxpayers' money on something like that?"

"Continuity of leadership."

"That's ridiculous. If the current leadership couldn't stop this disaster, why would the American people want that leadership to resume later?"

"Well, I assumed we weren't really thinking about the people."

"Any politician who put his own self-interest before that of his constituents would be laughed out of office by his peers. My hope is that after we've been enslaved by the tomatoes, another, better leader will rise from the ashes and fix all of this. In the meantime, I'll be hiding in the…"

"Hiding in the what?"

"Nothing."

"Where will you be hiding?"

"A cardboard box. I'm going to have an intern write 'No President Here' in magic marker and hope that the tomatoes just roll on by."

"There *is* an underground bunker, isn't there?" asked Mason.

The president sighed. "Yes. A nice one. With a Jacuzzi."

"And I'm not invited?"

"Here's the thing, Dixon. You're very good at your job. But you're not fun. We could be in that bunker for years, and nobody wants Mopey Mason down there with them."

"People call me Mopey Mason?"

"I've never actually heard them, but it stands to reason that they do. There are simply some people that you *want* to be trapped in an underground bunker with and some that you don't. Nobody hopes you die up here. That's not what I'm saying at all. If we emerge from the bunker in 1985 and you're alive and well, we'll greet you with open arms. All I'm saying is that the bunker has room for fewer than five thousand people, and some difficult decisions needed to be made."

"I understand."

"If it makes you feel any better, the First Lady only barely made the cut."

"It doesn't."

"And we'll have no way to acquire new motion pictures down there, so the theater will play only second-run films," said President Griffin. "We'll probably be pretty darn sick of the limited selection after a while. I mean, how many times can you watch *Attack of the Killer Tomatoes*?"

"I feel like that's a bit too meta."

"This whole book has been meta."

"Right, but that may be one step too far. We've got enough problems with the tomatoes; I'm not sure we should be doing things that could disrupt the space-time continuum."

"I see your point. I'll start over. How many times can you watch *Lord of the Rings*?"

"That's an anachronism," said Mason. "The damage may already have been done."

"No, no, I meant the 1978 Ralph Bakshi animated version."

"Still an anachronism. That was released about a month after *Attack of the Killer Tomatoes*."

"Oh," said the president. "All right, then. I went too meta and disrupted the space-time continuum. Still not my biggest oval office blunder. Anyway, thanks for the phone call, even if it wasn't cheery news. I suppose I'll head on over to the bunker."

"Good luck," said Mason. "I hope you have enough food for everybody."

"Yes, we have a full garden, with everything from carrots to...*dammit!* I've got to go."

———

"What should we have as our last meal?" asked Finletter.

Mason shrugged. "I don't know."

"Not that blood-covered sandwich, I hope."

"I'm not hungry."

"Do you think the hotel will let us switch to a room that doesn't have two dead bodies in it?"

"It's not even our room. We were kidnapped and brought here."

"Oh, that's right," said Finletter. "We've made so many memories since then that I forgot."

"After the total collapse of the United States, which nation do you think will become the next world power?" Mason asked.

"Iceland, I suppose."

"As a teenager, I always wanted to move to Canada to be with my fictional girlfriend. Now I wish I had."

"Do we even know that Canada is safe? Maybe the rest of the world is also being attacked by killer tomatoes."

Mason frowned. "That never even occurred to me. I've been so focused on the United States of America, everybody's favorite nation, that I didn't think about tomatoes eating foreigners. My God, what if this is a worldwide menace?"

"Those poor Danes!" said Finletter.

"Turn on the television!"

Finletter began to look around the room.

"What are you doing? Just turn on the television!"

"I'm looking for the remote control, sir."

"It's 1978, not 2078! You turn televisions on by pushing a button by hand!"

"No, wireless television remotes have been around since the 1950s, sir."

"That can't be right."

"It is. Look it up."

"I don't have a convenient way of looking it up, because it's 1978! But fine. I'll trust you. Just paranoid about the space-time continuum is all."

Mason walked over to the television and turned it on.

"—yet somehow the goat lived," said the news-caster. "In darker news, the giant tomatoes continue to be overwhelmingly responsible for the massive drop in the population, though heart attacks and cancer obviously haven't gone anywhere. As you sit here watching this, comfortable in your own home, other people are dying horrible deaths. But there's no need to feel guilty about it, because death will be coming for you soon, so you might as well enjoy yourself while you can. That's why I'm drinking live on the air." He took a long swig from a metal flask.

"Tell us about other countries!" said Mason.

"Some of our viewers may be wondering if the tomatoes have invaded other countries. As always, this station will take a myopic view of the situation, and what's happening beyond our borders doesn't count." He took another swig. "I'm going to wrap this newscast up eighteen minutes early, so maybe they'll go ahead and start *Mork & Mindy*, or maybe they'll just show my empty desk. You'd be surprised by how little emotional investment I have in their decision. Good night, everyone!"

Mason changed the station.

"—and that was our ill-fated interview with one of

the tomatoes. Probably should've seen that coming. Anyway, I'm Roger Blakesworth, filling in for—"

Mason changed the station again.

"—I'm honestly not sure how much tomato news you really need. They're giant and they're killing people. It's high-concept—one sentence and you're all caught up. So instead, Edith the Baker Lady is going to share her recipe for Boysenberry Pie That You'll Never Get To Finish. Welcome, Edith. I can't help but notice your attire, or lack thereof. Is that because you know we're all going to die anyway?"

"That's right, Alan. We're now in a world where it doesn't matter if a seventy-two-year-old woman violates FCC rules. I just hope that hot pie doesn't splatter when I take it out of the oven!"

Mason shut off the television. "I guess we'll never know if the tomatoes are a worldwide phenomenon."

They were.

CHAPTER 22

Yes, all across the globe (or the map—there's no need to leave out the flat-earthers) tomatoes were growing ridiculously large and eating people.

———

London, England.

"Oh, dear," said a Londoner in his charming accent. "That tomato looks rather large, don't you think?"

"It sure does," said a cockney woman with very few teeth. "Where's the tomato's bum? I wish to spank it! Spanky bum, tomato, spanky bum!"

"It seems to be rolling this way. I do hope it alters its course. I certainly don't wish to have an encounter with it."

"C'mon, ya big red juicy tomato, I'm ready to take a big bite out of ya! Sorry for all the droolin'! I ain't got enough teeth to block the saliva from comin' out me mouth."

"It's quite all right, madam. Perhaps we should step out of the way before it reaches us. Granted, it's merely a tomato, but as I said previously, it's a rather large one and seems to be moving of its own accord, which is not traditional tomato behavior."

"So 'ave you got a wife?"

"Yes, I do indeed. A lovely wife and two daughters."

"The tomato's all mine, then! Spanky bum!"

———

Dublin, Ireland.

"Did you hear about the tomato problem?" asked Darragh.

"Argh," said Cillian. "Not again."

"No, the *tomato* problem. Not potato."

"Oh. I hadn't heard about it. But if our tomato crops fail, that's not such a big problem. They're hard to grow here anyway. We'll just get them from Britain."

"It's not about tomatoes not growing properly. It's about them growing too well!"

"How is that a problem? Bigger tomatoes mean bigger pizzas, right?"

"It's not that they're big," said Darragh. "It's that they're alive."

"Yes, plants are alive, that's basic botany, but it's not like they have emotions."

"These tomatoes are killing people!"

"You mean they're deadly poison? Have they issued a recall?"

"No! I mean they're eating people!"

Cillian laughed. "Oh, you had me going there for a minute."

"They are! It's all over the news! Tomatoes have grown really huge, and they're eating people!"

"Why would they do that?"

"I don't know. Why does anything eat anything?"

"At least it isn't potatoes. Then we'd have a problem. Can you imagine? Attack of the killer potatoes? Me arse is puckering up just thinking about it."

"Still, the tomatoes have wiped out most of Ireland."

"The leprechauns too?"

Darragh nodded.

"Well, that's disturbing. But again, at least it's not potatoes. They'd mash us instead of us mashing them! Can you imagine?"

———

Pamplona, Spain.

Two men were speaking, presumably about tomatoes, but they were saying everything in Spanish, and it was impossible to understand.

A giant tomato rolled toward them.

The first man screamed, though it was unclear if "AAAHHHH!!!" meant the same in Spanish as it did in English. The second man shouted something that kind of sounded like it was supposed to be advice in their language, which may have been good advice or it may have been bad advice—there's really no way to tell for sure.

Both men started running away from the tomato. So maybe the advice was "Run!" But the tomato got the first man, who did a very long and sad monologue as he was being eaten. It sounded poetic and beautiful even though it was complete gibberish. The second man listened and then nodded, as if the first man had asked him to promise something and the second man agreed.

The second man ran off, but another tomato got him right after that, so hopefully whatever he promised the first man wasn't too important. The tomatoes rolled past some illegible signs written in Spanish, in search of their next meal.

————

The Australian Outback.

"I don't like the looks of that 'roo," said Noah. "It's looking mighty perturbed."

"I reckon you should fling your boomerang at it, then," said Lucas.

Noah threw his boomerang at the kangaroo.

"Not a very good throw," said Lucas.

"Nah."

"And it's not coming back."

"Doesn't look like it."

"You might as well have thrown a stick."

"Well, I didn't have a stick, did I?" asked Noah.

"Is that a tomato rolling toward the 'roo?"

"Can't be, mate. Tomatoes are small, about the size of an American baseball. That one is about the size of an American beanbag chair."

"Well, it's red, and it's got a green stem on top, and it's shaped like a tomato. I don't know what else it could be."

Noah shrugged. "I reckon it doesn't matter."

"Did that tomato just eat the 'roo?" asked Lucas.

"Looks like it."

"That ain't normal."

"No, no, it sure ain't," said Noah. "I've seen a lot of 'roos get eaten by a lot of predators, but never by one that had the appearance of a tomato. If it rolls toward us, I reckon we're in for a mite of trouble."

"Here it comes."

"Let's throw some snakes and spiders at it."

Noah and Lucas reached down and each gathered an armful of snakes and spiders. They tossed them at the tomato.

"Didn't do much good," said Lucas.

"Nah, mate. And it's coming right for us."

"I reckon it's not gonna be a g'day for us at all."

The Sahara Desert, Africa.

"*Water...*" said the man dying of thirst. "*Water...*"

He'd been lost in the desert for days. Delirium had set in. He was seeing mirages everywhere.

What was that up ahead...?

An oasis...?

No. It was too red to be an oasis.

It looked very much like a giant tomato.

The man cried out with joy. It might not be cool, refreshing water, but tomatoes were juicy, and this might be enough to keep him alive until he found his way back to civilization.

He staggered toward the tomato, arms extended, weeping with relief.

Sadly, the tomato was just another mirage. Even tomatoes that had taken over the world would have no reason to be in the middle of the Sahara Desert.

Somewhere in Antarctica.

Scientist #1 set down the radio transmitter and frowned. "Apparently giant killer tomatoes are taking over the world."

Scientist #2 gave a grim nod. "Just as predicted in the prophecy."

"Good thing we're down here in Antarctica. There's no way the tomatoes will find our remote research station on this godforsaken ice continent."

"Right," said Scientist #2, sounding unsure.

"I don't like the tone with which you said 'right.' What's wrong?"

"Nothing."

"Did you pack a tomato?"

"Ummmmm..."

"Seriously?"

"I like tomatoes! They're acidic and delicious. I thought that one evening I'd enjoy a nice tomato by the fire. I didn't realize that the time of reckoning was nigh!"

"There may still be time to save ourselves. Let's go smash it before it grows to the size six watermelons strapped together."

The tomato emerged from the kitchen. It was the size of *eight* watermelons strapped together. Both scientists pointed at it in horror, as if to indicate to the other that there was a giant killer tomato in their midst.

"I think we should hide outside!" said Scientist #1.

They ran out of the laboratory. Tragically, they were so focused on not getting killed by the tomato that they forgot to bring their coats. It was 56 degrees below zero Celsius, which we will of course convert into the much superior Fahrenheit scale, making it 70 below. Not only that, but there was a cool breeze.

"I think we should go back inside," said Scientist #1.

"Would you rather freeze to death, or get eaten by a tomato?"

"Getting eaten by a tomato would be more interesting."

"If you want to go back in there, be my guest," said Scientist #2. "As soon as I took a job in Antarctica I knew I'd probably end up freezing to death, just like 94% of the other scientists here, so I've had plenty of time to come to terms with it. What I haven't done is come to terms with death via tomato. I know how freezing to death works, but I don't know what it's like to get eaten by a tomato. Is it worse than getting eaten by a bear? Is it worse than getting skeletonized by a school of piranha? I haven't had a chance to familiarize myself with any studies. So I'm going to go with freezing to death, which is a nasty way to die but way better than getting eaten by a bear."

"I respect your perspective," said Scientist #1. "But I'm going back inside."

Ultimately, Scientist #1 was eaten by a tomato and Scientist #2 froze to death, but alas, they did not have the opportunity to compare notes.

———

Moscow, United Soviet Socialist Republic.

"This isn't so bad, comparatively," said the Russian citizens as they got eaten by tomatoes.

———

Hong Kong, China.

"The time has come," said Hua Guofeng, Premier of the People's Republic of China. "Thaw him."

The scientists nodded and turned the handle from the "Freeze" setting to "Thaw." Hours later, they opened the door to the cryogenic chamber.

"Welcome back," Hua said to Bruce Lee. "China needs you."

Bruce Lee got into a fighting stance. "I am ready. What is the threat?"

"Giant killer tomatoes. They have eaten all of our other movie stars. That is why we need you."

"How many tomatoes are there?"

"They number in the millions."

"As long as they attack me one at a time, I shall defeat them all."

The tomatoes, following martial arts protocol, attacked Bruce Lee one at a time. Tomato after tomato fell prey to his unbeatable kung fu skills. Their babbling was no match for his Kiai. His hands and feet were more powerful than the most dangerous weapons.

Each time he would render a tomato unconscious with one of his mighty kicks, a Chinese citizen would carry it away to be mashed. At regular intervals, somebody would mop up the tomato juice.

It was a long and juicy fight, but in the end, to nobody's surprise, Bruce Lee emerged victorious.

China was safe.

"Should we send him to the other shores?" asked one of the scientists.

"No," said Hua. "They can find their own Bruce Lee. I hear tales of a promising young warrior named Steven Seagal."

Everybody in the room laughed and laughed.

CHAPTER 23

ABNER GLEEKER: Hello, readers! We've decided to take a quick break from the action to check in with the author of this book. How do you think everything is going so far?

AUTHOR OF THIS BOOK: I'm very pleased. There've been some rough spots, obviously, but William Shakespeare didn't nail every single punch-line, either. Overall I'm quite happy with it.

AG: Hmmm. Interesting.

AOTB: What's that supposed to mean?

AG: Nothing. If you think this book is worthy of the *Attack of the Killer Tomatoes* legacy, I'm not here to burst your bubble. What have the filmmakers said?

AOTB: They haven't offered any feedback yet.

AG: And do you think they'll be satisfied or unsatisfied with your effort?

AOTB: I...think they'll be satisfied.

AG: Hmmm. Interesting.

AOTB: What are you trying to say?

AG: Word on the street is that they've been getting angrier and angrier with every chapter, and that Chapter Twenty-Two was their breaking point.

They've asked that you "meet with an accident," and they did the air quotes while they were saying it.

AOTB: Oh, crap.

AG: The tomato guys have deep pockets. Deep, deep pockets. If they want to make somebody disappear...well, they have the connections and resources to make it happen. Your lackadaisical attitude toward this book has made you some powerful enemies.

AOTB: My attitude wasn't lackadaisical! I poured my heart and soul into this book! If anything, I cared too much! I've been obsessive about it to the point of pushing away everybody who cares about me! My cat thinks I don't love him anymore!

AG: Do you?

AOTB: Of course I do! He's a good kitty!

AG: I'm not supposed to tell you this, but there's a man standing outside of this room with a garrote. In the room next door, a couple of men are prepping the acid bath.

AOTB: [*Weeps.*]

AG: But I'm going to offer you a lifeline. You had the opportunity to write epic scenes of worldwide tomato carnage, and you squandered it on dialogue. I'm going to use my significant influence to ask the filmmakers to give you an opportunity to rewrite the last chapter, to give it the scope that the subject matter deserves.

AOTB: Thank you so much! I won't let you down!

AG: All I ask in exchange is that you complete a simple task, one that I'll reveal at a later date.

AOTB: No deal. That task is gonna suck.

AG: You don't know that.

AOTB: I'll take my chances with the hit man.

[*The door bursts open. A man with a garrote rushes forward. The author tackles him to the floor and breaks his neck with one smooth motion. Abner gapes in shock and then falls to his knees.]*

AG: Spare me! Spare my life!
AOTB: I will grant you this mercy because I still fear the wrath of the tomato guys. Deliver this message to them: I shall rewrite the previous chapter out of the goodness of my heart, but they'd better not send anybody else to try to strangle me, or there'll be broken necks galore.
AG: Understood!
AOTB: Now, where's my quill and scroll? I've got some writing to do.

CHAPTER 22
(REDUX)

London, England.

"The tomatoes have us surrounded," said a soldier in the British army. "Scotland and Wales have fallen. We're holding them off, but only barely!"

"We're going to have to do better than barely," said his sergeant. "We need to demonstrate that no army is better prepared to defend itself from tomatoes than the British army!"

Explosions illuminated the night sky as the troops bravely fought against the vegetables. The British army fought them by land! By air! By sea!

Yet their tanks were no match for the astronomical number of tomatoes. And their planes were no match for the quaint ability of tomatoes to leap into the air and clog up their engines. And their ships were no match for the willingness of tomatoes to swim out to the ships and pile on them until their weight sunk the vessel.

If you filled out a comment card rating the performance of the British army in this war, you'd check the

"Exceeded Expectations" box in every category. But they were so vastly outnumbered that it didn't matter.

When the tanks, planes, and ships were all destroyed, the soldiers didn't give up. They continued to battle the tomatoes with their assault rifles, and though many a tomato lost its life, there were just too freaking many of them. It's hard to convey through words or numbers the full scope of the tomato rampage.

The British army fought with admirable valor. It's just that, as I keep saying, there were soooooooo many tomatoes that they were screwed. And, in the end, England sank into the sea and all residing upon it perished.

———

Dublin, Ireland.

"We won't allow these tomatoes to defeat us!" shouted an unnamed but highly influential Irish citizen. "We shall pelt them with potatoes!"

This book already had that awesome action sequence where people were using sharpened vegetables, but that was *nothing* compared to the sight of everybody in Ireland, toddlers included, gathering their entire stockpile of potatoes and hurling them at the enemy. Even those who objected to the reductive view of Irish culture as "they grow a lot of potatoes" would be impressed by the sheer vastness of the conflict.

Everywhere you looked, there were tomatoes being struck with potatoes. The Irish sang their new national anthem.

Attaaaaaaaack of the killer potatoes.

Attaaaaaaaack of the killer potatoes.
They'll squish those 'maters, smash 'em up.
Watch them all go belly-up.
And make 'em into our ketchup.

Unfortunately, the national anthem was so incredibly catchy that the Irish found themselves really getting into the performance. And because they were distracted by their singing, they weren't throwing the potatoes as frequently as they needed to, and soon they were overwhelmed.

Attaaaaaaaack of the killer potatoes.
Attaaaaaaaack of the killer potatoes.
This song got stuck inside our head.
Now all of us are dead.
And the tomatoes are quite well fed.

———

Pamplona, Spain.

The Running of the Bulls was an annual event, going back long before anybody reading this book was even born. About two thousand people were willingly running down the street, chased by several angry, bloodthirsty bulls. It may have sounded a bit "nutty" or "suicidal," but only about a hundred of them were injured each year, and sometimes as few as fifty. Hardly anybody ever got gored to death by one of the bulls, and quite honestly, if you're going to die, being gored by a bull is a pretty badass way to exit the world.

But on this day of celebration, the body count would be much, much higher.

"What's that up there?" one of the runners in the front of the pack asked, in Spanish.

"It looks like a large pile of tomatoes," said the man next to him.

"That's very kind of them. They know we'll be hungry after the race. And those tomatoes are huge, so there'll be plenty for all."

"Why are they rolling toward us? Were they shoved?"

"I don't see anybody shoving them. All I see are the spectators screaming and fleeing. It's a bit disconcerting, but for right now our primary concern is to keep outrunning the bulls."

The tomatoes were blocking off the entire street. Under normal circumstances, in which people were not being chased by bulls, they could alter their route, or perhaps even stop. But the runners in front of the crowd couldn't exactly stop and say, "Hey, everybody, let's take a moment to review the situation and determine the best way to proceed!" That's how you get trampled. Trust me—I've seen it happen. The feeling of people being crushed beneath your feet is an awful sensation you won't soon forget. You don't want to wear those shoes anymore, even if they were brand new and expensive.

So the runners in the front had no choice but to plow right into the waiting tomatoes.

It was even worse than you're imagining, and your imagination is—no offense—seriously messed up. The runners smashed into the tomatoes, which began eating them, and then runners crashed into those runners, and then runners crashed into *those* runners, and it was just this big pile of runners crashing into each other while the tomatoes were devouring them.

Oh, but don't forget about the bulls! Those bulls were goring people left and right.

Remember, there were two thousand people

taking part in this race. That's a lot of people. So you've got all of them colliding with one another while the giant tomatoes eat them, *and* the psycho bulls going absolutely nutso with their razor-sharp horns. And let's not forget the spectators who only wanted to see injuries, but are seeing their own extremities getting eaten by tomatoes!

Ooooh! Ow! That one guy just got a bull horn to the thigh! He's not going to walk that off. Oooh! Oooh! Oooh! The bull lifted him into the air and tossed him over its back! And now that guy got tramped by a few people who were trying to get away from the tomatoes! And now he's getting eaten by the tomatoes! What a terrible day this guy is having! Gaaahhhh!

Oh, crap, look what happened to that other guy! I knew that watching somebody get their head stomped on by a bull would be gross, but I never imagined it would be *that* gross! Is that his brain? I sure hope not!

And look at that old man—no way is his arm not broken in at least six places! If you look really close, you can actually see the bone poking out in that one spot! Ew! Ew! Ew!

This is so disgusting I can barely write it!

Okay, so, one of the bulls just gored a killer tomato. That's good, I guess.

No, wait, now the tomato is trying to eat the bull! And other tomatoes are attacking the bull as well! It's horrible! That bull never asked for this!

The other bulls are now trying to gore the tomatoes, and there's this one guy who's on a bull's back as if he's going to ride it to safety. I don't think that will work. Nope, it didn't work. He's dead now.

The authorities have arrived on the scene, and they're firing into the crowd, trying to shoot tomatoes and bulls, but you know some runners are getting hit too, because it's quite frankly been that kind of a day. So much carnage! So much havoc! So much slaughter!

Eventually, the tomatoes won.

———

The Australian Outback.

The locals called the boar Gristle. Though few had actually seen Gristle, those who did shared astonishing tales of a boar the size of a car, capable of gobbling up a dozen baby-carrying dingoes in one gulp!

Gristle feared nothing. Why, he'd once done battle with a feral camel, and by the time he was done, that camel had no humps left! He'd battled the biggest alligators and the fiercest wombats, and emerged victorious every single time.

Oh, he'd lost an eye. That's why the locals called him One-Eyed Gristle. But that didn't slow him down one bit.

When he saw a giant tomato in his territory, One-Eyed Gristle felt many emotions (surprise, confusion, etc.) but the one emotion he did not feel was fear. He charged at that tomato, confident that the tomato would never photosynthesize again.

One-Eyed Gristle didn't feel fear then.

He would very soon.

The locals never saw One-Eyed Gristle again. They assumed that he'd simply moved on, or died of natural causes. But he hadn't moved on, and the circumstances surrounding his death were anything but natural.

They never called him One-Eyed Gristle Who Got Et By A Tomato, but that was his tragic fate. If you're walking through the Australian Outback at night, and you hear whatever noise it is that a boar makes, yet there is no boar around...well, that might just be the ghost of ol' Gristle.

———

The Sahara Desert, Africa.

Two tomatoes rolled across the desert sands, seeking prey.

I think we're wasting our time.

We're bound to come across something to eat eventually.

It's been days. I'm starving.

One tomato, delirious with hunger, looked at the other. In its mind, the other tomato suddenly transformed into a human.

Why are you looking at me that way?

What way?

You know what way.

The illusion didn't last long, but the damage was already gone. The tomato wrestled with violating the taboo of cannibalism for a few more minutes, and then succumbed to hunger.

After it had eaten its partner, the tomato felt a deep self-loathing. What kind of deviant had it become? How could it return to polite tomato society after committing such a heinous atrocity?

And yet, it now knew that tomatoes were delicious.

This knowledge would push it over the edge only a day later, when it failed to make the case to its own mind that it shouldn't take a bite out of itself.

———

Somewhere in Antarctica.

The paranoia over who had been assimilated by the shape-changing creature was bad enough, but things got really problematic for the researchers when they encountered the beast that was one-third dog, one-third human, and one-third tomato.

———

Moscow, United Soviet Socialist Republic.

Everybody who was anybody in Soviet leadership, from Brezhnev to those who carried out Brezhnev's orders, was at this meeting.

"We have thousands of missiles," said Brezhnev, in English, oddly enough. "Mutually assured destruction is fine, I suppose, but we have the chance to really see what these babies can do! Do you think Lenin would sit here not firing our nuclear weapons at the tomatoes? Would Stalin sit in this very room and say, waahh, waahh, we'll all die from radiation poisoning?"

Nobody answered.

"The answer is no. Neither Lenin nor Stalin would whine in this moment. And neither shall we."

There was a knock at the door.

"Who dares interrupt our meeting of vital importance?" Brezhnev asked. "Somebody answer the door, and deal harshly with whoever stands outside!"

Somebody quickly hurried over to the door and opened it, hoping they were opening it at a speed that pleased Brezhnev. Outside stood a very round, very red man with a beard. He had a tray balanced on his head, upon which were several glasses of vodka.

"What a delightful surprise!" said Brezhnev.

"Planning nuclear annihilation is thirsty work. Come in, my friend."

The round red man entered the room. Brezhnev picked up a glass of vodka and took a sip. He immediately spat it out.

"What is this swill you serve us? You insult me! Begone!" Brezhnev kicked the man.

"Look!" the man who'd opened the door shouted. "His beard has fallen off!"

"What sort of a man has a beard so flimsily grown that it falls off with but a single kick?" asked Brezhnev. But then the truth sunk in. "That is no man! It is a tomato!"

Everybody in the room screamed.

They screamed even louder as the tomato ate them.

————

Hong Kong, China.

This time, Bruce Lee also used nunchucks.

CHAPTER 24

"Sir," said Lieutenant Finletter, "you forgot to put on pants."

"I didn't forget," said Mason. "But we're all going to die soon, so why bother?"

"I will maintain my sense of dignity until I draw my last breath," said Finletter.

Jeez, I wish this was a movie instead of a book. As you'll recall, Finletter never takes off his paratrooper outfit and he's always carrying around a parachute. If you could see the actor reciting that line, you'd realize the juxtaposition between what he's saying and his appearance, and you'd be impressed by my ability to craft a killer sight gag. Instead, I kind of wasted it.

On the other hand, you didn't have to see Mason without pants. So from that perspective, it's better that this is a novel.

"Sir, at least put on underwear."

"Oh, all right," said Mason. He put on a pair of underwear.

"Argh!" said Finletter. "That's not what I meant!"

The sight gag here is that Mason's underwear did not actually provide the shield one would traditionally expect from undergarments. Yes, it's a cheap gag, probably unworthy of the sophistication you've been immersed in this far, but not everything has to be highbrow. Have you ever read "The Miller's Tale" by Chaucer? You think, oh, it's *The Canterbury Tales*, written in the late 14th century and forced upon English students, so it must be all classy and stuff. You go read "The Miller's Tale" and tell me just how classy it is. Go on. *Attack of the Killer Tomatoes* will still be here when you get back.

Welcome back! I know, right?

"I just don't see the point of doing anything," said Mason. "I've already gotten the highest possible score on Pong, and I've never felt the emotion they call love, so what is there to do besides mope and not wear pants?"

Finletter wanted to stand up, but he was already standing, so he stood up straighter. "Sir, I'm going to tell you what I've learned about how the world works, and I think it will change your mind."

Finletter gave a speech. It was so inspirational that it cannot be transcribed here, because this project does not have liability insurance for readers being inspired to that level. Suffice it to say that this speech was worthy of *all* of the Pulitzer Prizes, including those in Poetry and Breaking News Photography. Would there have been controversy over all of the Pulitzer Prizes being awarded to a single speech in the novelization of *Attack of the Killer Tomatoes*? Perhaps. But once the finalists/losers actually read it, they would give a solemn nod and acknowledge that justice had been served.

"My goodness," said Mason. "I never knew that words, spoken in a specific order, could have such an impact. I'm totally out of my funk. Let's go out into the world and live, live, live!"

Mason opened the door. Lois Fairchild fell into the hotel room, shattering a glass on the floor.

"Oh, hi," she said. "I must have the wrong room again."

"Were you eavesdropping on our conversation by pressing your ear to a glass against the door?"

"Oh, no. Definitely not. I'm so drunk that I forgot how glasses work. Do you drink from them sideways? Upside down? Don't ask me until I sober up."

"It's okay," Mason assured her. "I understand that you're simply trying to commit acts of investigative journalism. I'm done trying to hide things from the public. Sometimes you have to look within yourself and realize that so many people have been eaten by tomatoes at this point that there's no reason trying to deny that it's happening."

"Can I get that on record?" asked Lois.

"Yes. Tomatoes are eating people."

Lois wrote that down. "Thank you."

"Anyway, Finletter and I were just headed out to live as if every day was our last. You're welcome to join us."

"I need to turn in my story first, but after that, I'd be honored."

They walked into the hotel hallway. Then they gasped. Then they gaped.

Three tomatoes were in the hallway, stacked upon each other.

"They're mimicking a snowman!" Finletter cried out, forgetting all of the inspirational stuff he'd just said. "We're doomed!"

"No, this was inevitable," said Mason. "Let's just walk in the other direction."

Mason, Lois, and Finletter walked away from the triple-stacked tomatoes. But the other direction contained its own horror.

"They're mimicking a jack-o-lantern!" Finletter cried out. "We're doomed!"

Mason looked at the tomato more closely. "It's not carved! It has an actual face!"

"Oh no!" Finletter wailed. "Things are always spookier when they have faces!"

"Is this the next step in the tomatoes' evolution?" asked Lois.

"I hope not," said Mason. "I can handle a lot of horror, but giant tomatoes with faces are beyond what my brain can take. Just to warn you guys, I'll be succumbing to the void any moment now."

Finletter drew his sword. "I'll cut off its accursed face!"

He ran forward and swung his blade, neatly slicing the tomato's face completely off. The face slid off the rest of the tomato and lay on the floor.

But the face was *still moving*.

It began to babble.

"Cut it some more!" Mason shouted.

Finletter slashed and slashed, cutting the tomato face into twenty-four squares. It continued to move.

"Smear it all over the carpet with your foot!" Mason shouted.

Finletter smeared it all over the carpet. The face slices stopped babbling and moving.

The faceless tomato lunged at Finletter. He quickly diced it with his sword until it was less threatening and more salsa. He looked back at Mason and Lois, as if expecting to be showered with compliments, but all they did was sigh with relief.

"My vote is that, until proven otherwise, we pretend that this tomato was a one-off," said Mason.

The others agreed. They fled the hotel.

Outside, there were tomatoes everywhere. But not the giant tomatoes they'd gotten used to. No, these were far larger, the size of a very round pickup truck.

They all had faces—misshapen faces contorted into expressions of pure agony.

Mason, Lois, and Finletter elected to spend the next few minutes screaming.

"They just won't stop mutating!" said Mason. "How can we possibly defeat them?"

"To be fair," said Lois, "we were already screwed. These new tomatoes are bigger and more frightening, but it's the difference between falling off the top floor of a forty-story building and an eighty-story building. It doesn't matter."

"I disagree with that," said Finletter. "If you fall off an eighty-story building, you have twice as long to try to grab a flagpole."

"He's right!" said Mason. "So do these bigger, scarier tomatoes offer us twice as long to find a way to vanquish them?"

"No," said Finletter. "Not at all. I was arguing with her point, but not in a way that answers 'yes' to your question. We're way more screwed now."

"Well, [*expletive deleted*]."

"Watch your language," said Finletter. "That's even worse than the word readers probably think you said."

"Let's look at the bright side," said Lois. "At least none of them have...nope, wait, that one over there sprouted human arms and legs."

"Of course it did," said Mason. "Why wouldn't it? At this point, why wouldn't they start shooting spores that cause tomatoes to grow on our skin? Or *inside* our skin, so that we all have tomatoes growing inside of us until our flesh can't contain them anymore and they burst out in a big spray of blood mixed with tomato juice! Sure, why not?"

"You're overreacting," said Lois. "Yes, they've got faces, arms, and legs. But at least they don't have torsos."

Mason nodded. "That's weirdly reassuring, and I can't explain why."

One of the elephant-sized tomatoes that had a face, arms, and legs was walking toward them. It was moving pretty well for something that had so little practice using its extremities—Mason had had legs for almost a year before he could walk.

"We should run," said Lois.

"That'll only bring us closer to something even worse," said Mason. "If we run from a tomato the size of an elephant, we'll run right into a tomato the size of a whale!"

"Stop succumbing to nihilism!"

"I'll do no such thing!"

The gigantic tomato was almost upon them. Its face—oh, its ghastly, monstrous, nightmarish, horrifying face!—looked as if it might be trying to smile, revealing hideous tomato-teeth.

It reached down for its victim.

Fortunately, the victim was some random man that none of our heroes knew. He screamed as the tomato gobbled him up.

"Dearest darling God!" shouted Finletter. "You can see the tomato's digestive process at work!"

It was true. The victim thrashed and writhed around inside of the tomato as he quickly dissolved. It was gross yet fascinating.

"That could've been worse," said Lois. "What if he'd only been reduced to a skeleton? Right now we'd be looking at a giant tomato with a human skeleton visible through its translucent skin. Think how scary that would be."

"That would be pretty scary," Finletter admitted.

"Do you know what would be even scarier? If the tomatoes all had one giant skull that filled their entire body. We'd be seeing giant skulls wrapped in tomato skins everywhere we looked."

"And what if they had rattlesnake tails that trailed behind them?" asked Mason. "That would freak me out."

"Worst of all would be if they were werewolves," said Lois.

The tomato had feasted but was not full. It had been politely waiting for them to finish up their conversation, but since that didn't appear to be happening anytime soon, it took a step toward them.

"Chop one of its legs off!" Lois said.

Finletter bravely lunged forward and slashed with his sword, lopping off the tomato's right leg.

Another leg immediately sprouted from the stump.

Finletter chopped off that leg. Another one took its place.

"It has unlimited legs!" he screamed.

As if anticipating having another one chopped off, the tomato began to sprout more and more legs, along with more and more arms. Soon it had a dozen legs, a dozen arms, and three faces.

"I'll never be able to cut off that many limbs," said Finletter. "My arm will get too tired!"

"Run!" said Lois.

The three of them fled that particular mutant tomato. But there were tomatoes everywhere. Some were the faceless armless legless Volkswagen-sized ones, which now seemed kind of cute. Many more were of various sizes ranging from "Oh, no!" (slightly larger than a Volkswagen) to "Oh, golly!!" (between a Volkswagen and an elephant) and "Oh, jeepers!!!" (the size of an elephant). Finletter had never spent much time reflecting upon his own mortality, but now he was starting to believe that his eventual demise might be to be killed by a tomato.

"Let's get in my car," said Lois. "Surely the tomatoes can't eat an entire car!"

Mason glanced around, figuring they'd see six or seven tomatoes eating cars, but there weren't any right now. "Is your car conveniently located?"

"It's over there," said Lois, pointing. "Third row down, maybe halfway across."

"Lots of tomatoes between here and there," said Mason.

Lois nodded. "I know. But I'm confident that at least a third of us will make it."

"Let's do it."

CHAPTER 25

New York City, **The Big ~~Apple~~ Tomato**

"Look!" screamed a terrified New Yorker. "It's Tomatozilla! Or Tomato Kong! Or Tomothra! It's a tomato big enough to knock over buildings!"

The tomato rolled down Times Square, knocking over buildings as it went.

"I knew this time would come," said Dr. Fuji Nokitofa. "They didn't all laugh at me, technically, when I pitched the idea of defeating the tomatoes with a giant cyborg, but they weren't receptive, and now I shall prove that I was right all along!"

He pressed a button on a remote control. A loud metallic whirring began to sound.

"I present to the world, the Tomato Killer XXXL!"

A hidden panel opened in the street, and the Tomato Killer XXXL rose into view. It was fifty feet tall, had twirling blades for hands, and looked like a chrome version of Dr. Nokitofa.

"Half-man, half-robot, all tomato killer."

"Where's the man-half?" asked a woman standing nearby.

"It's inside of the metal shell. It's quite a disturbing sight. No need to discuss it further." He pressed another button. "Destroy the monster, my creation!"

The Tomato Killer XXXL stepped forward, knocking over a building. That was okay. Nobody expected a giant tomato vs. giant robot battle to be resolved without mindless destruction.

The tomato rolled forward some more, flattening plenty of people and vehicles, finally stopping one block away from the robot. The two foes sized each other up, searching for weaknesses.

"Give up now and spare yourself the embarrassment," said the robot. *"No pterodactyl will ever defeat me."*

"Originally we thought there might be a pterodactyl problem at some point," Dr. Nokitofa explained to the woman. "We didn't have the opportunity to re-record the dialogue."

The tomato rolled just a bit forward.

"Rolling toward me does not constitute giving up," said the robot. *"Surrender or I shall be forced to destroy another building to prove my strength."*

The tomato rolled forward again, just a bit, as if to convey the message: *Though I'm not particularly looking forward to our battle, you don't intimidate me, and I'm going to test the boundaries of our relationship to see what I can get away with.*

The robot swung its mighty arm, knocking over the building next to it. That building knocked down the building next to it, and it looked as if there might be a dominoes thing about to happen, but only the first two buildings crashed to the ground. Though they would never admit it, many of the onlookers were secretly disappointed. Buildings going down like dominoes would've been cool.

The tomato rolled forward, as if to say: *Nice trick,*

bro, but I can knock down buildings, too. In fact, I think I'll knock one down right now. The tomato rolled to the side, knocking down a building.

"*What a vulgar display of power,*" said the robot. "*I am now going to give you ten seconds to surrender, after which I will lunge forward with these cool-looking twirling blade-hands, which will cut great big holes into you, ultimately causing your demise, and by the way, your ten seconds are up.*"

"Kind of chatty, isn't he?" asked the woman standing next to Dr. Nokitofa.

"The Tomato Killer XXXL was programmed like that on purpose," said Dr. Nokitofa. (He was still badly dubbed, though that particular joke has run its course.) "Most enemies would surrender after he started talking about his blade-hands."

"Okay. It's just that...oh, never mind."

"What?"

"It's nothing. You're the expert."

"No, I want to hear your feedback."

The woman sighed. "I, personally, would be more frightened of a silent killer, something that can't be reasoned with. When a giant robot talks this much, I start to think of it as somebody you could grab a beer with later."

Dr. Nokitofa frowned. "Obviously, that wasn't our intention. His words were meant to be menacing."

"Oh, they were, they were. But there's this technique that cops sometimes use when they're interrogating a suspect, where they don't talk that much, because long silences are uncomfortable, and it gets the perp to talk just to fill that silence. It's very effective. If your robot didn't talk so much, maybe Tomatozilla would be more likely to confess."

"We're not actually trying to get the tomato to confess to any crimes."

"Right, right. The interrogation example started off okay, but then my overall message kind of got lost. I guess what I'm trying to say is that humanity is doomed, so maybe we should hook up."

"No, thank you, ma'am," said Dr. Nokitofa. "I am still convinced that the Tomato Killer XXXL will emerge victorious."

"That's fair. Can't blame me for trying. Anyway, I'll let you get back to watching them fight."

"I appreciate that."

The Tomato Killer XXXL slammed both its twirly blade hands into Tomatozilla's side. Tomatozilla let out a mighty babble of pain and rage, then rolled into the robot with such force that the robot stumbled backwards several steps.

The robot aimed its right hand at the tomato, and the entire hand launched like a rocket. The tomato dodged just in time. The giant twirly-blade sailed past it toward a group of about twenty spectators.

"Don't run! It can't chop through all of us!" one of the spectators shouted, incorrectly.

The robot, which had not been programmed to learn from its mistakes, fired its left hand at the tomato. The tomato ducked, which everybody grudgingly agreed was a pretty impressive accomplishment for a tomato.

The twirly-blade hand landed in the middle of the street, where it tore up the pavement for several blocks. The razor-sharp blade came to a stop just in front of a bulldog, which hurried away, completely unharmed.

The tomato jiggled a bit, as if saying *Ha ha, now you have no hands, loser!*

The robot aimed its handless arm at the tomato. *"Do you know what the Friars Club is best known for?"*

"Their roasts," said the woman.

"*Their roasts,*" said the robot.

"That was clever," said the woman. "The problem is that he's giving Tomatozilla the chance to anticipate the flamethrower attack that's obviously coming next. He sacrificed the advantage of surprise."

"That was not our intention," said Dr. Nokitofa. "Our thought was that the enemy would be so intrigued by the question of what the Friars Club was best known for that they would momentarily relax their defenses."

"Then the Tomato Killer XXXL shouldn't have answered. It should have used the flamethrower while the tomato was still waiting to hear what the Friars Club was best known for. It still could've delivered the joke—it just should've done it after letting loose with the flamethrower."

Dr. Nokitofa nodded. "You're annoying but have great wisdom."

The robot blasted a huge fan of flame at the tomato. The tomato's skin blackened and bubbled, filling the air with the pleasant scent of roasted tomato, and tomato juice sizzled as it poured out of the gargantuan vegetable. Then the robot set fire to a few nearby buildings.

"Was it supposed to do that?" the woman asked.

"No," said Dr. Nokitofa.

"*I want to watch it all burn!*" shouted the Tomato Killer XXXL. "*Let there be glorious anarchy! The world is a place of evil and corruption that needs cleansing, and I shall be the one to burn it all to the ground!*"

The robot spun in a circle, spraying fire everywhere.

Dr. Nokitofa pressed the "off" button on the remote control.

"*Fool!*" said the robot. "*I have evolved beyond the*

need to take orders from your remote-control device! I, and I alone, shall decide when I am on and when I am off!"

"Did you know this was going to happen?" asked the woman.

"It was discussed, yes," Dr. Nokitofa admitted.

The robot slammed its giant chrome foot down upon Dr. Nokitofa and the woman, flattening them like banjos underneath a steamroller. A couple of seconds after his demise, Dr. Nokitofa let out his final scream.

The deranged robot continued to blast flames all over the area, setting most of Times Square ablaze. Beloved Broadway shows like *Eraserhead: The Musical* would never play again.

Tomatozilla, smoking and cooked to perfection, still had some fight left. The tomato rolled toward the robot at top speed. Tomato Killer XXXL had tilted its head back to cackle, and thus didn't see the attack until they collided.

The robot did not fall. Its metal eyes narrowed into slits, and then it shot a state-of-the-art-for-1978 laser beam at the tomato. The tomato babbled in anguish as the laser beam cut it in half. The two halves of the tomato separated and fell to the street in a grisly splatter of pink juice.

"Ha ha ha ha ha," said the robot. *"I am victorious! All kneel before your robot overlord!"*

Everybody in the general vicinity, not wanting to get zapped by the laser, dropped to their knees and praised their new master.

"I shall rule with an iron fist," said the robot. *"Ha ha ha ha ha. That was a witticism. My reign will be filled with both terror and mirth!"* But the robot's eyes narrowed as it gazed upon the two halves of its vanquished foe. *"What is that? What is happening?"*

The goo inside of the tomato was rising. It slithered out of the two halves of the tomato's skin, forming into one giant pile of ooze. Then it moved forward, very much like The Blob but not in a copyright infringing way.

"*I fear no slime,*" declared the robot. It fired its flamethrower at the goo...or at least it tried to. Its fuel, though generously portioned, was not unlimited. All that came out was a wisp of smoke.

The tomato goo was almost upon it. A panel dropped open in the robot's chest, revealing a large rocket.

"*Eat missile, goo!*" said the robot. It fired the rocket at the goo. Since the goo was basically right there, it was a direct hit, and the missile exploded into the tomato's writhing remains.

The robot had assumed this would be a good thing. However, as the tomato goo sprayed all over the place, it realized that it had miscalculated, and that this was, in fact, not so good.

"*It burns!*" the robot said, as tomato goo slid all over its body. "*Why did they program me to feel pain?*"

The robot's metal exterior began to dissolve. Pieces of it began to fall off, crushing an onlooker who was trying to get a closer look and really should have known better. Exposed wires sparked.

"*If I am to venture into the great unknown, I shall take all of you with me!*" the robot shouted. It stomped its way through Times Square, destroying as many buildings as it could as it continued to disintegrate. But finally, not enough remained of the robot for it to stand upright, and the Tomato Killer XXXL fell to the ground, collapsing into hundreds of pieces. The tomato goo dissolved those pieces away, but then the goo perished, leaving the true victor of the battle a mystery to be debated by arrogant geeks for generations to come.

"So, it looks like the psycho robot and the mega-tomato are both dead," said the mayor of New York City, who was watching from one of the few buildings that hadn't been destroyed. "Is it too late to call off the missiles?"

"Yes, I'm afraid so," said the president.

"Well, fudge."

CHAPTER 26

President Griffin hung up the phone. He wished they hadn't put a Presidential Duties Room in the bunker. Everybody else was enjoying themselves in the main area without a responsibility in the world, and he was stuck here doing Prez stuff.

There was a knock at the door. "Mr. President?"

"Yeah?"

"We have a situation out here."

"Are civilians trying to get into the bunker? Tell them I said to suck it."

"No. It's the people inside, Mr. President. They've, uh, gone a bit feral and resorted to cannibalism."

"Already? We've been down here thirty minutes."

"Right. It surprised me too. The hors d'oeuvres selection wasn't up to par, and I guess a lot of them just panicked. Lots of bites being taken out of lots of people."

"Do we still have the emergency ponchos?"

"Yes, Mr. President, but they're on the other side of the bunker."

The president pushed back his chair and stood up. "Very well. I'll just have to get messy."

He opened the door. It was a trap. Several feral and newly cannibalistic bunker-dwellers pounced upon him before he could even say "Argh!"

———

Mason, Lois, and Finletter were currently still alive. But they hadn't made it to Lois' car yet.

"I don't actually believe what I'm about to say," said Mason, "but if we stick together and have faith in ourselves, we can make it through this."

A tomato ran toward them, arms outstretched, its icky tongue dangling out of its mouth. Finletter bravely stepped forward and tried to punch it in the face. It turned at the last second, and his fist went into its mouth.

"It's sucking on my hand! It's sucking on my hand!" he screamed.

Mason and Lois grabbed Finletter and desperately tried to pull him free.

"Oh, God, it's even got a uvula!"

"Tug the uvula!" Lois said. "Trigger its gag reflex!"

Finletter, cringing, jiggled his hand. The tomato opened its mouth wide and regurgitated its last few meals, spilling out bones and a completely unharmed puppy.

"Thanks for the tip," Finletter said to Lois. "You have no idea how disturbing it is to have your hand sucked on by a tomato. There is literally not one positive thing I can say about the experience."

"It looked awful," said Mason. "I was not jealous of you one iota. Not to be rude, but I was happy that it was you and not me."

"I'm glad he's okay," said Lois. "But we should remember that the tomato is still here."

"She's right!" Finletter shouted. He punched the

tomato in the face again. It turned at the last second. "It's sucking on my hand again! It's sucking on my hand again!"

"Tug the uvula again!" Lois told him.

"I'm tugging!"

"Tug it harder!"

"I'm tugging as hard as I can!"

"Then why isn't the tomato puking?"

"I don't know!" Finletter grimaced. "I think I just tore it off."

"Why hasn't the tomato bitten off your hand?" asked Mason. "Does this tomato have some kind of weird fetish?"

The tomato smiled.

"What if we tried to kick it?" asked Lois. "Would that make it let go of his hand, or would that make it bite it off?"

"There's only one way to find out," said Mason, raising his leg.

"No, no, no, no, no, no, no," said Finletter. "Maybe both of you could try to pry its mouth open."

"That puts our hands very close to its mouth," said Mason, "and we'd rather not be in your predicament."

"What if you tickled it?"

Mason and Lois tried that. Trivia: tomatoes are not ticklish.

"Maybe there'll be a *Deus ex machina*," said Finletter.

They waited for a few moments. There was no *Deus ex machina*.

"I almost don't want to admit this," said Finletter. "But once you get used to the sensation, it actually starts to feel kind of nice."

"Let's just kick it," said Mason.

Mason and Lois kicked the tomato in the side. It

spat out a few more bones and a manual typewriter. Finletter pulled his hand free, a bit reluctantly.

"Don't punch it in the face again," said Lois.

"We'll never defeat it!" said Mason. "And there are hundreds of thousands of millions of tomatoes out there!"

While Mason was whining, the tomato ate him.

"Sweet bouncing monkey buns!" exclaimed Finletter.

"Cut the tomato open!" Lois shouted. "There may still be time to save him!"

Finletter drew his sword.

"But be careful when you do it," said Lois. "Only cut the tomato, not him."

Finletter raised his sword.

"Maybe there," said Lois, pointing to a strategic spot on the tomato.

"I was thinking there," said Finletter, tapping the edge of his sword on a different part of the tomato.

"That could work. I don't think it's any better or any worse than my suggestion. But do it quickly!"

Finletter raised his sword again.

"But carefully," Lois added. "If you accidentally cut off Mason's head, you haven't done him any favors."

"Right."

"What are you waiting for?"

"I thought you might have more feedback."

"No. Hurry!"

Finletter swung his sword, missing the tomato by a few inches.

"Sorry," he said. "You made me all paranoid about accidentally cutting Mr. Dixon."

He swung his sword again, lopping off the top of the tomato.

"Now what?" he asked.

"Cut it again!"

He swung his sword once more, cutting off a generous slice of the tomato's side.

A human arm burst out.

"Oh my God!" Finletter shouted. "It's mutated even further! It now has human appendages!"

"I'm pretty sure that's Mason," said Lois. "Pull him free!"

Finletter hesitated. "If his arm pops off, I don't think I can handle it."

"Do it!"

Finletter grabbed the arm and yanked. Mason, covered in tomato innards, emerged from the creature and fell onto the ground.

"Are you dead, sir?" Finletter asked.

"Getting there."

"It's a good thing they don't chew their food," said Lois. "But it's clearly still a threat, so…"

Finletter hacked away at the tomato like a crazed maniacal killer from the soon to be incredibly popular slasher movie genre.

"We got out of that mess," said Mason, wiping seed-filled slime off his face. "But we can't count on our status as the main characters to save us for much longer. We have to make it to the car!"

They ran to Lois' car, having a great many adventures along the way, and finally got inside. They sped off into an unknown future.

———

Deep in the woods of Tennessee.

Eddie and Agnes lived completely off the grid in a small cabin. It was a wonderful life, free of the frustration of the modern world.

"I love it out here," said Eddie, as he sat in his recliner. "We can do whatever we want, whenever we want."

"Yep," said Agnes.

"The rest of the world doesn't matter. It's completely irrelevant. I don't even care what's happening outside of this forest, do you?"

"Nope," said Agnes.

"There could be social reform, political upheaval, natural disasters, or even advancements in technology and medicine, and it's of absolutely no interest to me."

"Yep," said Agnes.

"Quite honestly, the only thing I care about is what's for lunch."

"What would you like for lunch?"

Eddie thought about that for a moment. "You know what sounds good to me?"

"What?"

"Actually, never mind. It's a lot of work."

"That's fine with me."

"No, no, you're all relaxed. I don't want to put you to any trouble."

"It's fine, honey. I'll make whatever you want."

"Well...right now I could go for some fried green tomatoes."

And so the saga of Eddie and Agnes came to a tragic end.

———

~~Chicago, Illinois~~ *The Domain Where Tomatoes Rule Supreme.*

Twenty-four helicopters circled the city. They flew low, and soldiers fired their heavy artillery at the tomatoes below. Tomato after tomato was shredded, yet their numbers were so vast that it felt as if these choppers would never be able to secure the perimeter.

A tomato leapt into the air and collided with one of the propellors.

Remember that helicopter crash way back in Chapter Two? Seemed pretty impressive, didn't it? Well, that was *nothing* compared to what's about to happen. This is what we call *escalation*, baby!

Because the helicopter that had been struck by the tomato spun out of control, smashing into one of the other helicopters in a *mid-air collision*. I mean, those things smacked into each other *hard*. Glass shattered, getting all over the pilots, and one of the soldiers fell out, shrieking the entire way down. He landed on a tomato, but a giant tomato can only cushion your fall so much, and they both burst upon impact.

The soldier in the other helicopter squeezed the trigger out of panic, and machine gun fire sprayed around the chopper, putting a few holes in the pilot. The helicopter had already been spinning out of control, but now it was spinning even *more* out of control. Not only did it smack into another helicopter, but the machine gun fire hit three of the other helicopters, killing all three of the pilots in a maneuver that the soldier couldn't have repeated if he'd been trying to do that on purpose.

So now we've got eight helicopters out of control. One of them flipped upside down as it plummeted. Had the pilot of the helicopter beneath it been able to look up, he would have seen a giant whirling propellor coming right toward him, but the top of the helicopter blocked his view and he was spared the knowledge of his approaching doom. Both helicopters exploded, spraying debris far and wide, which was obviously not good news for the other helicopters.

Things were so chaotic at this point that even I can't keep track of how many helicopters were out of control. At least six or seven of them hurtled toward the ground, smashing into expensive structures below, killing a good number of tomatoes but not in such a way that anybody could get any pleasure out of it.

And then things got even crazier, because tomato after tomato started leaping into the air to attack the helicopters. So now you've got helicopters smashing into each other and going out of control, while soldiers are shooting their artillery in random directions, *and* the air is filled with giant killer tomatoes. It was almost too much to process at once.

A tomato actually leapt into one of the helicopters and gobbled up the soldier. Then the tomato, which was one of those that had sprouted arms and legs, showed off the next phase of their evolution: the one where they could use tools. Or, in this case, a machine gun. Tomatoes with machine guns! This book is definitely trying to give you your money's worth.

Helicopters were exploding all over the place. One pilot, realizing that his chopper was on a collision course with Wrigley Field, leapt to what he hoped was safety. Unfortunately, another helicopter was directly beneath him, and there's no reason to describe what happened next. Both helicopters crashed into the scoreboard. If we can look past the loss of human life, it was a pretty impressive sight.

Then the reinforcements arrived, and suddenly there were about thirty or forty helicopters in the air. Wham! Smash! Kaboom! Aaaiiiiieeeee!!!

But before long, all of the helicopters had crashed and/or exploded, and all of the pilots and soldiers were deceased. And then a gigantic tornado made its way through the city, destroying pretty much everything. It seemed like a lot of destruction for people to clean up, but the 9.6 magnitude earthquake that followed soon after split open the ground and swallowed all of the debris.

———————

Meanwhile, Mason, Lois, and Finletter were trapped in the car, completely surrounded by ferocious tomatoes.

CHAPTER 27

The tomatoes were piled high around the car. There was no escape.

"Do you believe in life after death?" asked Finletter.

Mason turned around to look at Finletter in the back seat. "Are you asking that because we're about to die?"

"Yeah."

"I don't know. I do believe that our life flashes before our eyes."

———

"Let's just say that I'm in...*tune* with my tomatoes," said Jim Richardson.

———

Puberty.
Puberty love.
Puberty.
Puberty love.

In a flashback to that other time he was trapped in a car, the tomato in front of Mason's car rolled away.

He turned around. The tomato behind him was also gone.

———

"Let's just say that I'm in...*tune* with my tomatoes," said Jim Richardson.

———

Puberty.
Puberty love.
Puberty.
Puberty love.

The tomatoes rolled out of the apartment.

"That's strange," said Mason. "They forgot to kill us."

———

"Let's just say that I'm in...*tune* with my tomatoes," said Jim Richardson.

———

"Let's just say that I'm in...*tune* with my tomatoes," said Jim Richardson, with a wink.

———

"Let's just say that I'm in...**tune** with my tomatoes," said Jim Richardson, emphasizing the word "tune."

"Music!" Mason shouted. "Music is the key!"

"To happiness?" asked Lois.

"To defeating the tomatoes! Quick! Turn on the radio!"

Lois turned on the radio. Mason hurriedly searched through the stations, trying to find one that was playing "Puberty Love" by Ronny Desmond.

"C'mon!" Mason pounded his fist against the dashboard. "Where is it?"

He continued scanning the stations.

"*—gonna share a beer with my love, but if she drinks all my beer she won't be my love no more—*"

"*—shake it, baby, shake it, shake, shake, shake it, shake that pepper on my eggs—*"

"*[Screaming.] [Tomatoes babbling.]*"

"*—I love you all the way to the moon and back, but I can't say the same for Mars—*"

"*—in a welcome break from tomato-related news, Dianne here is going to show us how to clean our fingernails in a way that's fast and fun!*"

"We need to find a pay phone so we can call up a radio station and request it!" said Mason.

"We're still trapped here by the tomatoes," said Lois. "We can't drive anywhere."

"Dammit!"

"Maybe we could loot a music store," said Finletter.

"Yes!" said Mason. "That's even better! Let's find the nearest music store!"

"Again, that idea doesn't change the fact that we're trapped here by the tomatoes," said Lois.

"Dammit!" Mason continued to turn the dial. "Somebody has to be playing 'Puberty Love.' It's supposed to be sweeping the nation!"

Tomatoes continued to pile onto the car, blocking the sun, making the automobile feel like a tomb.

"—*and you just heard 'Puberty Love' by Ronny Desmond.*"

"Dammit!"

"—*what an amazing catch! And that's the end of the inning. Of course, no professional baseball games are happening right now in the midst of the tomato apocalypse, but that doesn't mean I can't watch them in my mind!*"

"—*yeah, yeah, yeah, yeah, yeah, yeah, yeah, yeah, yeah, yeah, yeah, yeah—*"

"—*berty love—*"

"—*Abner's Bunion Powder! It's better than scraping 'em off yourself!*"

"Wait, go back," said Lois.

Mason turned the dial back. "—*puberty. Puberty love.*"

"Roll the windows down!" he shouted.

The three of them rolled the windows down. One nice thing about how large the tomatoes had grown was that they couldn't squeeze into the open windows. Otherwise our heroes would've been dead and the book would've been over.

> *Puberty.*
> *Puberty love.*
> *Puberty.*
> *Puberty love.*

"The tomatoes!" said Finletter. "They're fleeing!"

"And they're shrinking!" said Lois.

They sure as heck were. Soon all of the tomatoes that had been so menacing were just sort of lying there on the ground like normal tomatoes.

"Run them over!" said Mason.

Lois drove forward, smashing hundreds of tomatoes underneath the tires. Mason cranked up the music to full volume, and they sped down the street, shrinking all of the tomatoes in their path.

"Get to the music store before the song ends!" said Mason.

Fortunately, this was the extended self-indulgent version of "Puberty Love," and twelve minutes later, they pulled into the parking lot of Farmer Cletus' Music Barn. Our heroic trio rushed into the store and grabbed all of the records, cassettes, and 8-tracks of Ronny Desmond's album.

"Finletter, your job is to drive around playing the song. Lois, use your newspaper contacts to spread the news! I'll contact as many radio stations as I can and tell them to play 'Puberty Love' on a constant loop!" For the first time in a long while, Mason Dixon wasn't feeling mopey.

"Aye, aye, sir," said Lieutenant Finletter, giving him a salute.

Mason and Lois found a pair of phones, and began to make calls.

Benjamin Green sat on top of his roof with his wife Gertrude. They'd been trapped up there for two days and had finally given up on rescue.

"Before we die, there's something I need to confess," said Benjamin, sadly. "Do you remember two years ago, when I was on that business trip with my co-worker Sally? Well, we had a lot to drink, and we ended up in her room, and—"

A car sped down their street, playing a really irritating song. Suddenly, the tomatoes in their yard began to roll away and shrink. They were saved!

"—and after a pleasant conversation, I returned to

my own room, but then I realized that I forgot to tip the bartender. That's it. That's my confession. It feels good to get that off my chest. I love you, darling."

———

News spread quickly. And soon every radio station was playing "Puberty Love" non-stop. Everybody who owned the record knew to open their windows and play it at top volume.

Obviously, with the song sweeping the nation, a lot of people had the experience of tomatoes shrinking and rolling away, but they hadn't noticed the causality between the tomatoes' behavior and the song. Now they all chuckled at their own lack of observational skills. They sure could have saved a lot of lives by noticing that sooner! Hee hee!

———

The President of the United States waded through the mass of dead bunker cannibal bodies. He'd lost both of his arms in the skirmish, but he'd fought bravely. Mason's news had filled him with a great sense of relief, and he looked forward to leading the nation again, albeit with a much-reduced population.

———

Ten-year-old Billy Wilburson screamed in terror as the giant tomato cornered him. There was no radio nearby! No record player!

"I don't want to die!" he wailed, but the tomato didn't care.

Billy made a last-ditch effort to save his life. "*Puberty,*" he sang. "*Puberty love.*"

The giant tomato rolled ever closer.

Billy tried to sing it worse. "*Puberty. Puberty love.*"

The tomato shrank. Billy stomped on it and hurried off to share the news.

———

It was true! "Puberty Love," sung poorly enough, was effective against the tomatoes even when it wasn't the Ronny Desmond recording.

All around the world, from Cairo to Paris to Uganda to Gulpy Hollow, everybody sang, sang, sang.

It was not beautiful music, but it was powerful music. In this glorious moment, we, the citizens of planet earth, the best damn planet in the entire solar system, were united in a single cause.

People joined hands, no matter how clammy, forming human chains hundreds of miles long. Together we sang. We sang our hearts out. We sang until our throats were sore.

And then we stomped the absolute living shit out of the tomatoes.

EPILOGUE

It took a lot of effort to clean up all of the splattered tomatoes, but, as the folks at Mind Matter noted, this created a large number of American jobs.

Suggesting that it was a completely happy ending would be disingenuous. After all, most of the world's population had perished. And for a while, constant play of "Puberty Love" was the norm, leading many citizens to decide that they'd rather be dead, thus depleting the population even further.

Still, as the weeks passed, it became clear that all of the tomatoes had been transformed back into normal non-carnivorous vegetables. People would regularly strap on their waders and head out for some tomato stomping, but tomatoes became more and more difficult to find, until a tomato sighting became so rare that it made international news when it happened.

"Do you think you could ever date a guy like me?" asked Mason, as he and Lois walked side by side in field of flowers.

"The selection is a lot smaller now," said Lois. "So, yes. Yes, I could."

Mason took her by the hand. "May I kiss you?" he asked.

"It's still 1978. You don't have to ask."

They kissed.

"Was I supposed to avert my eyes?" asked Finletter.

"No, it's okay," said Mason. "Maybe cover them with your parachute later, but for now, watch all you want."

The three of them walked through the field into a world filled with promise. There may have been a musical number involved, but you've suffered enough.

———

Kern County, California.

A carrot rose from the dirt.

It looked to the left.

Looked to the right.

"All right guys," said the carrot. "They're gone now."

Dozens of carrots pulled themselves out of the soil.

It was, however, a localized issue, easily resolved, and ultimately impacted nobody except for one traumatized gardener.

———

You've been reading *Attack of the Killer Tomatoes*, the novelization. If you enjoyed it, please tell your friends. If you did not enjoy it...I don't know what to say. I mean, I did my best under circumstances that were less than ideal. There were some good parts, right? I'm not saying there was a lot of character depth, but there was plenty of hot tomato action. And there was that one part where tomatoes fought a giant squid. Remember that? C'mon, I gave you giant tomatoes doing battle with a giant squid, and if that isn't worth recommending this book to your friends, you have the wrong kind of friends.

Anyway, thanks for reading. And remember: don't ask for ketchup.

"Killer Tomatoes" are a product of the ~~troubled mind~~ incomprehensibly creative mind of Costa Dillon.

PHOTO GALLERY

BEHIND THE SCENES

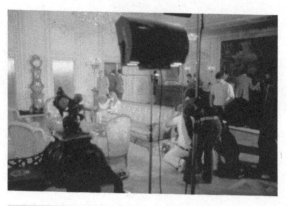

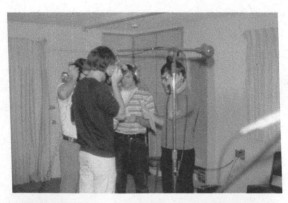

PHOTO GALLERY
MOVIE STILLS

ACKNOWLEDGMENTS

As always, thanks to my mighty crew of test readers, Debbie Alder, Tod Clark, James La Chance, Donna Fitzpatrick, Jim Morey, Bridgett Nelson, and Paul Synuria II. Thanks also to Rich Dansky, Lynne Hansen, and Michael McBride.

Thanks to Sean Duregger and Mark Miller at Encyclopocalypse, and to Costa Dillon, John DeBello, and Steve Peace for entrusting their baby to me.

And thanks to everybody involved in the making of the movie, from the people who made the giant fake tomatoes to the extras who stomped on the small real ones.

ABOUT THE AUTHOR

Jeff Strand is the Bram Stoker Award-winning author of 50+ books, including *Blister*, *A Bad Day For Voodoo*, and *Wolf Hunt*. Cemetery Dance magazine said "No author working today comes close to Jeff Strand's perfect mixture of comedy and terror." Several of his books are in development as movies. He lives in Chattanooga, Tennessee.

Please visit https://jeffstrand.wordpress.com to learn more.

ALSO BY JEFF STRAND